The
Falcon Sting

The
Falcon Sting

by Barbara Brenner

Bradbury Press
New York

An excerpt from C. P. Cavafy's "Ithaka" appears on page
13. Edmund Keeley and Philip Sherrard, trans.
C. P. Cavafy: Collected Poems. ed. George Savidis.
Copyright © 1975 E. Keeley and P. Sherrard. Excerpt
from "Ithaka" reprinted with permission of Princeton
University Press.

Bradbury Press
An Affiliate of Macmillan, Inc.
866 Third Avenue, New York, NY 10022
Collier Macmillan Canada, Inc.
First Edition
Printed and bound in the United States of America
10 9 8 7 6 5 4 3 2 1

The text of this book is set in 11-point Caledonia.
Book design by Julie Quan

LIBRARY OF CONGRESS CATALOGING-IN-PUBLICATION DATA
Brenner, Barbara.
The falcon sting.

Summary: Marina meets a troubled boy in her
creative writing class who shares her interest in
falcons and together they try to uncover a rare
bird smuggling operation.
[1. Falcons—Fiction.   2. Rare birds—Fiction.
3. Smuggling—Fiction]   I. Title.
PZ7.B7518Fal   1988   [Fic]   88-14567
ISBN 0-02-712320-0

*Thanks to Stephanie and Bill Streeter,
Randy Hale, Hope Carpenter, Linda Lee,
and all the other falconers and bird lovers
who shared their knowledge and
love of raptors with me.*

TO
FRED, MARK, AND CARL

CHAPTER

1

THE NAME OF THE TOWN IS SERENITY. IRONIC, considering what happened there.

But this April morning was *before*. Before the murder and the sting. Serenity was still living up to its name.

In the desert the wild residents went quietly about their business. Cactus wrens called softly from the cholla. Finches clustered like raspberry ornaments in the paloverdes. In the saguaros, Harris hawks hunched in friendly family groups, while above on the telephone wire red-tails and kestrels perched like statues, or took off in sudden graceful flight toward the distant mountains.

It was clear the hawks owned this land, even where the town began to encroach on the desert. There were only a few houses. One filling station. And the high school.

This particular Saturday about fifty of Arizona's young

people were gathered inside Arroyo High School, participating in a program the school district called Accelerated College Experience—ACE.

One student, at least, did not seem thrilled.

Marina Cassidy stared out of the window, watching the birds, as if it were unfair for them to be outside when she was inside, even though she was there by her own choice.

Marina couldn't quite put her finger on exactly what she was after.

She had tried telling Isabel.

"Growing pains," had been her mother's diagnosis. "It's natural. Have a little patience. Before you know it you will go out into the world, go away to college. Meanwhile, what you need, *chiquita*, are some new experiences. Seek them out."

So Marina had sought. And ACE seemed to be the closest thing to an experience Marina could find in Serenity. She applied and was selected.

Now, after only one session, she suspected her choice was a gigantic mistake. Not her fault. Not her mother's either. Marina knew at whose feet to lay the blame—Professor Arnheim's.

"Let me remind you," he was saying at this very moment, "writing skills are *ee-sential* for college entrance. Writing skills separate the chaff from the wheat—the Ivy Leaguers from those consigned to state schools and community colleges."

Gah! This was a writing teacher?

The thing to do is to relax. Make the body the vessel of the mind. I read that somewhere. Makes sense. So the cre-

2

ative juices can flow from brain to arms to fingers and from there to . . .

"And so, if we can manage to mobilize our full energies this morning . . ."

Marina narrowed her dark eyes to slits. She ducked her head down behind the computer monitor. That way she could see only half of Arnheim. And vice versa. She had already discovered it was fatal to creativity to make eye contact with Arnheim. He had a bad attitude problem. In fact, his bad attitude had probably already dried up most of the creative juices in the class.

The sharp-looking blond guy, for example. The one who sat in front of her with his big foot out in the aisle. There was nothing much going on at his computer. After the first class he had been up and out without so much as a glance at anything but the floorboards. Maybe he, too, sensed the danger of making eye contact with Arnheim.

Marina's gaze roamed back to the window. *I feel like Rapunzel locked in her tower, waiting to be rescued. No one made me come here, and I don't have to stay. Do I stay because I think maybe writing is the adventure I'm after?*

Write about what you know, Arnheim had said. It seemed a useful piece of advice, but was it really? There's not much to write about if nothing much has happened to you.

She took off the cover of her Bic. Try it with pen on paper first. She wrote:

Have you ever looked into a hawk's eye? Up close, I mean. It's like looking into a black jewel.

3

But fierce, too. Intense. As if each look were a matter of life and death. I guess it can be, for the hawk. Spy the quail or starve. See the lurking hunter or get shot.

The people of the Australian outback have a legend. They say everything in the world was sung into existence. So who sung up the hawks and falcons? Is there a different song for the red-tail, the Harris, the prairie, the sharp-shinned hawk? What tune called up the peregrine?

Marina stopped to read what she had written. What if Arnheim made fun of it, thought it was silly?

She crumpled the paper, aimed it at a wastebasket. *Swish!*

The blond boy lifted his head and watched the paper hit the basket in front of them. For a moment Marina was sure he was going to turn around. But instead he hunched over the keyboard again.

She shrugged. *That's that.*

What I know. Let's see. She knew Isabel. And Isabel was interesting.

Marina turned on her computer. The green cursor blinked like a little beacon light, urging her on.

My mother, Isabel, is a potter. But she makes her living as a caterer. Isabel says cooking is just another creative expression. She also says she can make more money from pots that have food in them.

4

Everything Isabel makes looks and tastes good. Her best catered dinner is a chicken mole with blue-corn tortillas. *Típico* Mexican. In fact, Isabel is half Mexican. And all beautiful, as my father used to say. He was an artist, too. A painter. Will was a wild guy. I remember once he saw a sketch that another painter had done. He liked it so he chewed it up and swallowed it. When Isabel asked him why he did it, he said he wanted to *digest* what the artist was trying to do!

Will died of a heart attack when I was nine. I remember everything about him but the way he looked. Now I think of him looking like his work— big and bold and colorful. We have a lot of his paintings. Isabel won't sell them even though we could use the money. She says she'd rather make a living catering and keep the paintings.

Marina paused again to read.

It had feeling, anyway. Maybe too much. But what if Arnheim asked where it was going? As if a story were some kind of a tour bus, taking you on a mapped-out trip.

I'm not going to give him the chance to pick at my parents.

She printed out the paragraph and put the printout in her desk drawer.

ARE YOU SURE YOU WANT TO CLEAR? the computer asked. YOU HAVE NOT SAVED THIS TEXT.

Oh, yes, I have. She pressed YES.

Her story disappeared from the screen.

Good. That was settled.

She thought for a minute, then smiled to herself and started again.

There's this muscular blond guy sits in front of me in ACE. I noticed him the first day. Gray T-shirt no sleeves faded jeans small V-shaped scar back of neck single earring. I think his name is Nick. Like a razor cut. Suits him, with that spiky hair. Anyway, when I'm trying to think of something to write seems like I always end up staring at the back of his head. Nothing personal. But I'm beginning to know the back of his head better than he does. Which isn't saying much since you don't get a chance to see the back of your own head that often.

I'd like to ask him how he got the scar and why the hair around it is white. But I don't have the guts. It's hard to get to know anyone in this class. Even the girls. Some are not from around here; they come from all over the district. All blonds. That's Arizona for you. I'm the only one with black hair in the whole class. I feel like a subspecies. *Homo sapiens hispano-americanus arizonius.*

He must be from outside. Never saw him in school. I would have remembered him because . . .

Suddenly Marina was conscious of a tinkling sound. She looked around the edge of her computer, beyond the bare muscular shoulders. The subject of her story was holding a pair of tiny leather straps to which were attached two small

6

metal bells. He was swinging them slowly back and forth.

For their size, the bells were remarkably loud. They insisted on attention. The click of computers stopped. All eyes turned toward the noise. At first the boy didn't acknowledge the silence. When he finally looked up, he was frowning.

"Sorry," he muttered in a sullen tone to the room in general. He turned and looked directly at Marina. His eyes— half-mocking, half-challenging—caught hers and held them for a split second. She drew in her breath. And then the moment was over.

He lay the bells down on his desk.

There was a slight flurry of giggling. Then the class settled back to work.

All except Marina. Had she imagined the look? She had to know more. She craned her neck. The bells were lying on the boy's desk. She could see the strips of leather attached to them. A memory began to tease her. Where had she seen bells like that before?

The boy had just begun to write something on his screen when the buzzer rang. He jumped up and made for the door.

Marina sat for a minute, collecting her thoughts. She saved her text, then cleared her screen. She stood up and gathered her papers together. As she did, she glanced at his computer screen.

He hadn't even cleared it. She couldn't help reading what he had written. One sentence:

The sound of her bells will always remind me of Roxanne.

Well. You had to admit that was a good beginning for a story. Intriguing. So who was Roxanne? Marina glanced down at the desk, as if somehow the clue might be there.

Then she noticed that he'd left the bells!

She snatched them up and ran from the room, hoping to catch him. But she got to the front of the building just in time to see a helmeted figure zooming down the road on a large black motorcycle.

Now isn't that perfect. He's definitely a motorcycle type.

She stuck the bells in the pocket of her skirt. *I'll return them to him next week,* she told herself. She tried to ignore her disappointment. She should have made her move sooner.

As she walked toward the bicycle rack, the old discontent surfaced again. Not a satisfactory morning. No new experiences. Not even a good story. She decided that the only way to rescue the day was to go out into the desert, and spend the afternoon hawk-watching. That's what Will used to do, when he wanted to get away from it all. Watch the birds and you ease the heart and mind, he'd say. Of all the birds, he had loved the hawks the best. She smiled. *Maybe there's a gene for hawk-loving, and Will passed it on to me.*

CHAPTER

2

MARINA FREED HER TEN-SPEED FROM THE bike stand, and started for home. If she hurried she'd still have half a day in the desert.

She pedaled along on the flat blacktop for about a mile. Then the hills began. She shifted gears. As she neared home, the slope became steeper. And at last she gave up, got off the bike, and walked.

The house sat on the crest of a hill, hugging the desert so closely it seemed almost to have risen out of the sand. Will Cassidy had built it with his own hands. He had mixed the adobe brick on the site, sculpted the fireplace and the built-in sofa, white-washed the walls and ceilings. Everything was his creation. He had even painted the jaunty sign of weathered wood that hung above the door: *Casa Cassidy*.

Marina wheeled her bike to a side entrance that opened onto a small inside courtyard.

"*Hola*, Isabel," she called. "I'm home."

A soft musical voice came from the kitchen. "*Hola, niña.*"

Marina went straight to her room to change. As she was taking off her skirt she heard the jingle of the bells. She reached into her pocket, took them out, and laid them down on the dresser. Later she'd think about them. Right now she wanted to get going.

She changed into chino pants and a plaid shirt, then tucked binoculars into a backpack and added gloves and a poncho. Spring in the desert seldom called for a poncho, but there was something about the sky today . . .

A little food and water and I'll be all set.

She followed the sound of music and the trail of good smells to the kitchen. Her mother was presiding over a worktable covered with bowls and pans, stuffing mushrooms in perfect time to a rock tune playing on the radio. She looked up and waved a spoon in Marina's direction.

"So how did the class go today? Better?"

"Well, I started a story about you. But—in general—I would say it went—" She made a retching noise.

"A simple yes or no will be sufficient," Isabel said quietly.

Marina changed the subject.

"Listen, Ma, I'm going out to do a little birding. I'll be home before dark."

Her mother's face clouded. "Remember, I need you tonight for the Menaker party."

"Uh-oh. I forgot. Yeah, well, don't worry. I'll be back in time. I'll just go as far as Montenegro."

Isabel started to say something, then seemed to think better of it.

Marina surveyed the inside of the refrigerator. "Any objection if I take some of those raw carrot and broccoli things and the guacamole dip?"

"No. Finish the dip. It'll turn brown. I made too much." Isabel sighed. "I must learn to be more cost-effective."

Marina helped herself to a small container of avocado dip and slipped some vegetables into a plastic bag.

Her mother continued to stuff mushrooms, but clearly she had something more than mushrooms on her mind. She spoke, choosing her words carefully. "You know, *niña*, I'm not happy with you going always alone out there to the desert. It used to be okay but lately . . . I've been hearing stories. . . ."

Marina frowned. "What's this, all of a sudden? I never see anyone out there. No one goes to the desert. They're all in the shopping malls. Now *that's* where you have to watch your step," she added, mock-serious. "Pickpockets, muggers, and rapists all over the place. Kidnappers, too. I heard that two girls disappeared from the South Mall while buying eye makeup."

Isabel Cassidy's eyebrows were eloquent. She spoke to an invisible judge.

"Don't mind her. My daughter has a poor sense of humor. She does not know about the criminal element. Kidnappers. Smugglers. Cocaine dealers. Who knows what they will think of to do next?"

11

"Well, if they don't think of a better way to run drugs than to cut through the desert, I don't have too much respect for them."

"Aha, smart alley cat. Shows how much you know."

"Smark *aleck*, Ma." Marina grinned. Even when her mother made a mistake in English, which wasn't often, she somehow managed to sound charming.

"Never mind that," her mother said. "Haven't you read in the paper how they steal Indian pots from the burial mounds, and saguaros from the desert? Everything is a business today."

She stopped for a breath before delivering her final thought.

"So you see what I mean. You are out there with all these bad people around. And with only the birds for company. I still say you are too much alone out there with your hawks and your desert. You should be more with kids your own age. Sometimes I wonder why we moved to such a deserted spot. I question the way we brought you up. I wish you were more like the other girls your age. Put a little makeup on, meet a nice boy, it wouldn't kill you."

Marina stopped foraging and prepared for battle.

"Well, now, this is a switch. Other parents are worried that their daughters are too involved with boys. You're worried 'cause I'm not."

Her mother looked pained.

"I guess I worry no matter what you do. I am a single parent. I have no one to share with about bringing up a daughter in today's world. So I worry. And lately you're so funny—up and down. One minute you are laughing, the next minute you cry or get cranky . . ."

"You think I'm cranky because I don't hang out with boys?" For an instant Marina thought of the boy in school. What if she told Isabel about him, asked her advice? Instead she said, "You're wrong. I mean, that's only part of it." She stumbled, trying to put her feelings into words. "I don't know who I am. I don't know where I fit. I'm not a junior deb valley girl, I know that. And I'm not into smoking dope and driving around in fast cars either."

"Are those the only two choices?"

"How do I know? I'd like to look around, try a few things on for size. Maybe I'll learn to write well, like you do pottery well. I need to find my own style."

Her tone changed as quickly as her mood. "Going into the desert is part of my odyssey, don't you see that? Weren't you the very one gave me that poem that Will had saved for me? You know, the one about Ulysses."

She stood in front of Isabel and recited the verses by the Greek poet that she already knew by heart.

When you set out for Ithaca
Ask that your way be long,
Full of Adventure, full of instruction . . .
The Laestrygonians and the Cyclops,
Angry Poseidon—do not fear them:
Such as these you will never find
As long as your thought is lofty—
As long as a rare emotion
Touch your spirit and your body . . .

"Now that says it all. I need adventure and I need instruction. I need to have a great walkabout, a wandering, an experience. And by the way"—Marina moved swiftly from poetry to argument—"how come you suddenly have such a yen for me to be like other girls? Were you and Will Mr. and Mrs. Average American?"

Her mother gave her throaty giggle.

Marina could see she had won this round, anyway. She indicated truce.

"Hey, *Madre*, don't worry about me. Okay?"

"Okay. I don't worry about you anymore. Who would want to bother you, anyway? You're prickly as the cholla. Even a rattlesnake would think twice before attacking you."

She stood up, hands on hips.

Just then the music stopped.

"We interrupt this broadcast to bring you a special news bulletin."

And suddenly there was a radio voice adding weight to everything Isabel had said.

"This morning a white Mercedes van crashed a border blockade near the town of Patagonia and escaped into the desolate mountain terrain of border Mexico. Authorities believe the van belongs to a ring of thieves that deals in rare and endangered wild hawks and falcons. The birds are being smuggled across the border into Mexico and shipped all over the world. Federal wildlife officials estimate that four to five hundred falcons have been captured and transported this way within the last year."

Isabel glanced at Marina, who was staring at the radio as if it were alive.

"You see," she said quietly.

Marina hardly heard her. She was still digesting the

news broadcast. It was weird that her mother's worries were confirmed so quickly. And doubly disturbing was the fact that the smuggling involved falcons. *Hawks. Her birds.* It *was* scary to think that there were people around who actually captured birds illegally for a living. On the other hand— Hey! You want excitement, adventure? Here it is! And then she thought, *How silly! It isn't happening here. Nothing is happening in Serenity.*

Her mother had clicked off the radio and was still talking to her, urging something. She tuned in to what Isabel was saying.

"Then you be careful. Maybe you shouldn't even go."

"Ma, that happened on the border. Hundreds of miles south of here. Forget it. Don't worry. I'll be careful."

"And one more thing . . ."

Marina mimicked what she knew was coming next.

"Protect your skin in the sun," she sing-songed, laughing. "Good-bye, Isabel."

She breezed out of the kitchen, grateful that Isabel had gotten back to trivial worries about her. She reflected on her sometimes stormy relationship with her mother. Discussions these days always ended in a standoff. Marina could never tell beautiful, talented, charming Isabel that she deeply admired her, was more than a little jealous of her, wanted to be more like her, but at the same time needed to be different from her. On the subject of boys, Marina felt clumsy and awkward, especially compared to Isabel, who managed to be fascinating to everyone without even trying. It was as if her mother knew a secret language and a way of being that Marina had not yet learned.

It was hard to tell Isabel her feelings about boys. *There*

are two kinds, she wanted to say. *The boys who don't interest me and the ones I'm afraid of. The wild, dangerous ones. Like that Nick, with that look in his eyes.* She couldn't say these things to Isabel.

Still, one piece of her mother's message had hit home. Marina rooted around at the top of her closet until she found a broad-brimmed old straw hat that would shield her from the sun. As she passed the mirror she caught a glimpse of herself. Clunky desert boots, old chino pants, faded Western shirt a little too short in the sleeves. She made a face. *This is finding your own style, kid?*

On impulse, she grabbed a handful of dried flowers and stuck them around the brim of the hat.

"You never know when you'll meet someone out there," she said aloud. So saying, Marina Cassidy stepped out her back door and into the desert.

CHAPTER

3

MARINA HEADED FOR THE BOULDER-STREWN hills. She wanted to check out the presence of a pair of falcons she had caught a glimpse of, just once, hovering above a remote cliff in the high desert. If she was lucky, they had been scouting the site and might be nesting about now. Finding a nest would be something for her to write about. Grist for the mill.

After I check them out, the rest of the afternoon is open. If the weather doesn't screw me up. The sky was still cloudless, but there was something in the air. Electrical storm, maybe? She tried to shrug off a slight feeling of apprehension.

Darn Isabel, anyway. Her worry agenda was catching. Marina gave herself a pep talk.

Hey. Don't let it spoil your good time. This afternoon is for relaxing and observing. Experience!

In the distance Marina could already see the piles of gray rock that were her destination.

A half hour of brisk walking and she had reached the base of a cone-shaped mountain of glacial boulders about seven hundred feet high. Montenegro, she called it. Black Mountain.

She took off the lens caps of her binoculars and prepared to scope out the territory.

She had just put the binoculars to her eyes when the falcon appeared, bursting into the bright blue Arizona sky from some unseen place above her head. Abruptly, it changed course and returned to the boulder cliffs. It flew straight up the face of the mountain as if to outrace the wind. Then it hung at high altitude, beating its sickle-shaped wings against the sky, hovering until a larger bird launched from the sheltering rocks to meet it.

The falcons wheeled in tandem, almost touching, rolling over, soaring, breaking apart and swooping together again in a breathtaking ritual sky dance.

Marina watched, spellbound. This was what she had come for—the hawks, but especially for the chance to glimpse a "longwing." Falcons are the nobility of the hawk clan.

Marina kept her glasses on the wheeling birds. *They're so perfectly made for what they do*, she was thinking. *They use themselves so well. No trying to find yourself, for a hawk. Everything is right there, bred in the bone. No wonder that in ancient times hawks symbolized higher consciousness.*

She trained her glasses on the sleek, streamlined

shapes. What kind of falcons were they? Was it possible they were peregrine falcons? There were probably only about one hundred and fifty pairs of them in the whole Southwest!

So why should they pick this spot? Then she remembered. Behind Montenegro was a small lake. Permanent water. If they were peregrines, they had taken up residence because their favorite prey, ducks, would be nearby.

It was pure romance. Two endangered birds that had found each other. Neat. Unless, Marina reminded herself, these two were bred in captivity and released here. Not as romantic but more scientifically plausible. *And still a serendipity that I get to see them.*

She heard a call like the sound of a rusty hinge. *Wichew.*

Soon one bird disappeared behind the rocks. Marina sensed that the remaining falcon was watching her as closely as she was watching it. Knowing raptor eyesight, Marina was sure the bird was getting the better view. Then the second bird disappeared behind the mountain. But not before the sighting had shaped Marina's afternoon. If there is a pair of peregrines performing mating dances in spring, there's the possibility of a nest. And where there's a nest there can be eggs, and then *eyasses*—baby birds—and the chance to observe and then write about the family life of birds. *It may not be high drama to Arnheim,* she thought, *but I love it.*

She decided to look for a nest. She knew where it would be. Up. Way up.

It was a daunting idea, to climb Montenegro. The cliff was both high and steep. There was no consistent trail, no footing. It was a matter of finding a space, taking a few steps, then looking for the next place to put your foot.

Well. Here goes. Marina pulled on her gloves and began to climb, working her way up slowly by grabbing one boulder and then another, pulling herself along. She was careful to look before she put her hands near crevices. Lots of critters, including rattlers, liked to hide in niches in the rocks. She had no desire to surprise anything at close quarters.

As Marina got higher it became harder to find footing and handhold. *Not so dumb, these birds. They make it tough. The ones that nest where anyone can find them don't last long.*

It was not a good idea to look down, but about halfway up she decided to stop and investigate what lay above. She braced herself against the rocks and looked upward. She was startled to see the silhouette of a large animal basking on a boulder. She felt a small flutter of fright. *Mountain lion?* No. *Rock squirrel*, she decided, and the biggest one she'd ever seen. As she watched, it slid silently from view. She resumed climbing and at last arrived at a place where she could look through the boulders to the opposite side of Montenegro.

But the vantage point was not good enough. She would have to get slightly above so she could look over and down. The peregrines' nest would be on a ledge, narrow and inaccessible. But she'd also have to stay far enough away so that they wouldn't spook. Not easy.

She started up again. Finally, near the summit, she found a sort of natural overhang on the sunny side of the mountain.

If there is a nest, she decided, it will be in shade now. They may be active. She braced herself and peered between the boulders. Not a sign of life. Even the rock squirrel had made itself scarce.

Marina sat down under the overhang. She waited for what seemed hours. Suddenly, without warning, she heard a noise—the harsh, begging cry of a female falcon. *I knew it*, she thought triumphantly. But where was it coming from? She stood up again, searched the rock face with the glasses. And then she saw it—the foot-long shelf of rock hanging dizzily out into space. On it there was a shallow depression, no more than a scrape in the rock, and around it the telltale debris—slivers of bird bones and the white "noodles" of typical falcon droppings. And last, but certainly not least, were exhibits A, B, C, and D: four mahogany-colored eggs, visible for the moment because the female was off the nest.

The male—the tiercel—returned first. Now Marina could see quite clearly the blue-black cap and mustache, slate blue back, buffy underparts barred with brown, and the characteristic sooty clown markings under its eyes. "It really is a peregrine," she breathed in a thrilled whisper.

And then the female—the larger bird—returned. Marina spun the focus on her binoculars madly, trying to get a better look. She couldn't believe what she was seeing. This bird was peregrine in shape. But instead of being slaty, the female was pure platinum white. Was this some breeder's fantasy? A hybrid? Or a true albino?

Whatever the biological reason, it was wildly unusual. One of a kind, probably. And the mahogany eggs in the nest might carry that silver-white gene. What a falconer

21

wouldn't give for this rare bird or its offspring! Marina's eyes went to the bird's legs. No band. It was a wild bird. Nature had done this, not some breeder.

Suddenly a gray shape with a three-foot wingspread hurtled toward her from above. So swift was the tiercel's descent that if he had attacked she would have had no time to defend herself. He swooped by, the wind from his wings a menacing whistle in Marina's ear. She was being warned. She was too close to the nest.

Marina knew the tiercel might dive again. But to move fast could mean losing her footing. She worked her way down as quickly as she could while watching her step. *Please*, she pleaded as she went, not sure what she was asking for or whom she was asking. She knew only that peregrines have been estimated to "stoop," or dive, at close to two hundred miles an hour, that they can deal death to prey with a single rap of their talons. This falcon could "bind" to her arms or even her head, digging into her with talons like giant fishhooks. But the great bird contented itself with flying at her. Then both peregrines ascended to hover high above her, watching with eyes that were capable of seeing the tiny beads of sweat forming on Marina Cassidy's upper lip.

When Marina was about halfway down the boulders, the peregrines left off their aggressive surveillance, as if satisfied to have driven her to her own eyrie. Marina paused at a wide ledge. She needed to stop for a few minutes and think about what had happened.

Marina sat back against the rock face of the mountain. She was breathing heavily and glad to be out of the sun for a few minutes. She took off her pack and rested it beside her. The water in the canteen was still cool. She drank, and then realized for the first time that she was hungry. She spread out the vegetables on a piece of waxed paper and opened the container of guacamole.

She dipped a carrot into the sharp-tasting green paste and chewed thoughtfully.

Things were looking up, experience-wise. She had made a double discovery: a peregrine falcon nest and what looked like an albino bird. Two wild falcons. Four eggs. And she was probably the first person to see them.

Marina sat reflecting happily for some time before she became aware of movement below her. Looking down, she caught the glint of sun on glass. There was something down there behind a clump of creosote bushes. Instantly uneasy, she moved back farther into the shelter of the rock. The conversation with Isabel surfaced, as if it were on tape.

The criminal element . . . Okay, smart alley cat . . . No one would molest you, you're too prickly . . .

And then she grinned in relief. It was someone wearing a suit of camouflage! What a *turkey!* Camouflage suits were for woods, where trees made dappled light and shadow. In the desert, chinos and tan shirts were camouflage, assuming you needed it. So therefore, Marina murmured, he is not from around here. Probably an Eastern dude, and certainly no one to be worried about.

She wondered what he was doing. Birding maybe.

You don't own the place. Other people can come here to watch birds.

23

At least he wasn't a "plinker," one of those weekend hunters. She saw no evidence of a gun. Maybe he was a falconer, scouting a nestling to train. Licensed falconers were allowed to take the young of certain species, like Harris hawks and red-tails. But not a peregrine eyass! She knew that much.

Reassured that she wasn't visible, Marina finished eating and put the waxed paper neatly back in her pack. Then she picked up her binoculars again and studied the stranger.

He wasn't wearing a pack, but he did have a canteen of water. At least he wasn't a complete idiot about the desert. He also seemed to have a very good pair of high-powered binoculars on a tripod. So maybe he *was* a birder, with professional equipment.

Her foot slipped and dislodged some rocks. They rolled down the hill. The stranger, alerted, trained his glasses in her direction.

Isabel's warning echoed, joined by the radio broadcast. Marina shrank back, pressing her body so hard against the rock that she could feel each ungiving lump of granite.

The stranger took a few tentative steps up the cliff.

Now that he was closer, Marina could see him better. She saw that he was short and barrel chested, and that his sunglasses sat on brown curly hair above a deeply suntanned face, rugged but not unattractive. *Kind of a Richard Burton type.*

He stumbled slightly as he climbed.

What is he after, anyway? I'm sure he doesn't see me. He isn't in good enough shape to climb these rocks.

But he kept climbing.

Marina started looking around for an escape route.

Her concern was interrupted by a clap of thunder. The sky had turned gunmetal gray. There was definitely going to be a storm.

She tried to decide what to do. If she made a run for it, she would have to put herself right in the path of the man. If she stayed, she might get wet. She decided to stay put.

She tucked herself as far back under the overhang as possible. A flash of lightning zigzagged across the sky. She counted: one thousand one, one thousand two, one thousand three . . . Thunder rolled. Three seconds between lightning and thunder. That meant the storm was less than a mile away. Meanwhile, it appeared that the stranger, too, had heard the warning of the impending storm. She watched him collapse his tripod and trot off in the direction of the road. Marina estimated he wouldn't be able to outrun the rain. She settled under her ledge, watching the lightning crackle and continuing her thunder countdown.

And then the smell of rain was in her nostrils. The downpour began. Soon she couldn't see anything but a wall of water. Marina knew that for a little while now the water would be in charge of life and death in the desert. Water would cascade down the arroyos, pouring over the rocks, seeping into the cracks on the desert floor to release the seeds that lay dormant, awaiting just such a moment. Lizards and small mammals would be caught in the torrent and drowned. When the water receded, the vultures, caracaras, and other carrion-eating raptors would have a feast.

She thought of the peregrine eggs on that narrow ledge. What a lousy break for them to be subjected to a storm like this.

Twenty minutes later the storm was over and the sun

25

was out. Marina slogged through the wet desert, headed for home. She felt elated, enriched. Bird-watching 101. It was the best course in nature's curriculum.

She didn't give another thought to the stranger.

CHAPTER

4

WHEN MARINA ARRIVED HOME HER MOTHER'S flamboyant pink Casa Cassidy van was parked in front of the house. Isabel was already loading trays and steel containers of food into the back.

Her mother's voice had a decided edge.

"Where the heck were you? I was *very* worried. We're running late."

Marina struck her forehead with her hand.

"Golly. I forgot about the party. And I got caught in the storm."

"What storm?" asked Isabel somewhat sarcastically.

What storm, indeed! Marina realized that the ground here was perfectly dry. It hadn't rained at Casa Cassidy at all.

"There *was* a storm up there," she said sheepishly, waving in the direction of Montenegro.

Isabel nodded acknowledgment of quirky desert storms, then said briskly, "Hurry up and change. You've got fifteen minutes."

"I'll help you load," Marina said guiltily. "I'll go as I am. I'll only be in the kitchen, anyway. Just give me a minute to wash up."

Isabel's glance took in the dirty chinos, the scuffed boots.

"No, I need you to help serve. We'll do this my way for a change. Get dressed in something decent. And pronto."

Isabel had slipped into her seldom-used tough voice. Marina knew that meant she'd better hop to. But she had to make one quick detour—to her bird book. Hastily she leafed through the pages on hawks. Nothing like it. No pale platinum hawk. So it must be an albino or a hybrid of some kind.

She would have liked to spend more time pinning down the identification. But Isabel was waiting.

Marina rushed in and out of a shower. She slipped into a Mexican skirt and an embroidered white blouse and sandals. Over her skirt she put one of the poppy-print aprons that were her mother's trademark. "But what do I do with this horse's mane?" she muttered, looking at her waist-length black hair. If she took time to rebraid it, they'd be late. She ended up brushing it hurriedly, tossing it over one shoulder, and looping the end up behind one ear with an elastic band. At the last minute she snatched up a red ribbon to cover the elastic.

Mercifully, Isabel did not comment on her appearance.

They rolled out of the driveway with minutes to spare, the van full of fragrant pans of appetizers, cold meats, huge bowls of salads, and rows of Chocolate Sinbads—the finger-size chocolate cakes that were one of her mother's delectable dessert specialties.

"So how was your birding today?" It was Isabel's way of declaring a truce.

Marina got the signal.

"Fine. Ma, I saw a pair of peregrine falcons and their nest. At least I *think* they were peregrines. But the female didn't look like any peregrine in the book."

"Hmm." Isabel negotiated a turn. "Your father used to see peregrines all the time when we first lived here. How he loved those birds! He said they were the most beautiful hawks in the world."

"I don't remember that we saw many when Will and I used to go birding. They got very scarce. DDT got into their food chain and made the shells of their eggs so thin that when the females sat on them, they'd crack. They're endangered now. The species, I mean. In the Northeast they're considered extinct. They're trying to bring them back with captive breeding. But I think the ones I saw today were wild."

"I see. Well, that's good," Isabel said softly. "Maybe they're coming back. And you saw no one? No bad guys?" she asked, as if laughing at herself.

"No bad guys." Marina suddenly remembered the man with the tripod. *At least I don't think so.*

She decided to say nothing. Soon Isabel turned in at a gate at the end of a long wall that surrounded a group of elegant houses. She drove around a spacious circle and stopped at a sign that said MENAKER.

"Here we are."

Marina looked around. She'd seen houses like this before. She and Isabel jokingly referred to the people who lived in them as the *ricos*—rich folks. There were the walls of purple bougainvillea, the citrus trees, the fragrant oleander around the Spanish-style courtyard. In the back would be the swimming pool, cleverly lit for maximum effect. The buffet would be set up in the dining room, facing the pool. Later in the season the parties would be outdoors, and the food would be served around the pool.

The host seemed tense, perhaps because there did not appear to be a hostess.

"I thought you'd never get here." He seemed about to say something else, but Isabel cut him off.

"Plenty of time," she said smoothly. Marina could almost see him relaxing as her mother proceeded to take charge.

Bravo, Madre, she thought admiringly, as she watched her mother find her way around the kitchen, introduce herself to the household staff, give orders in her quiet voice, and make everyone feel comfortable—all at the same time.

"And this is my daughter, Marina," she announced. "She'll help serve and keep me in touch with what's going on out front. She'll be responsible for reinforcements."

Some guests began to arrive. Marina knew from long experience what to do. She liked circulating with the plates of appetizers and emptying ashtrays. She felt invisible, eavesdropping and collecting tidbits of talk for possible stories.

"Boyd says he's always been a bit of a problem," she heard one woman say to another.

Boyd. Let's see. That would be Mr. Menaker. So . . .

"After the divorce he went completely out of control. Liquor, drugs, the whole bit. I heard he had an arsenal of weapons. Spent all his time hunting. Shot everything in sight. Took a bow and arrow one day, shot his mother's portrait smack through the heart. Now if that isn't symbolic, I'd like to know what is."

For a moment, Marina forgot why she was there and stood listening. It was only when the woman said pointedly, "I said no thank you, dear," that she remembered her duties. She moved away, but slowly, so she could hear the rest of the story.

"He finally got into real trouble with the law. Sure. They hushed it up. Terrible for poor Boyd. As if he didn't have enough trouble without a son who . . ."

Who what?

It was a small party, only a dozen people, and there was help with the dishes, so by ten o'clock Marina's chores were finished. All that was left was to pack up the van.

"I'm going outside for a little air, Mom."

"Okay, *chiquíta*. Just don't disappear." Isabel was in a corner of the kitchen taking compliments from two guests who had come back to ask her about the Chocolate Sinbads. Her mother was guaranteed a few new clients every time she made that dessert.

Marina stepped out the back door and into the fragrant spring night.

She stood at the head of the driveway and breathed in the scent of oleander. Clear night. Moon. Plenty of stars. Breeze rustling through the eucalyptus.

31

She could hear the guests laughing, the distant sound of a motorcycle.

The harsh burr of the motorcycle came closer, jarring the tranquility of the evening. It slowed at the end of the driveway, then roared up to the Menaker garage.

Marina stood unnoticed in the darkness. The rider cut the motor, pulled off the Darth Vader helmet. His face was clear in the moonlight.

It was Nick, the razor cut!

Marina stood quite still until he noticed her.

When he finally realized she was there, he got a strange look on his face.

"I'll be darned. Look who's here. The third computer to the left."

A small heart blip. He *had* noticed.

They stared at each other for a minute. Then Marina said, "What are *you* doing here?"

"I live here. What's your excuse?"

Be cool.

"I'm helping my mom. We catered the party tonight."

The boy swung his leg stiffly over the motorcycle seat.

"I'm Nick Menaker," he said abruptly, holding out his hand.

"Marina Cassidy." Marina tried to be casual, but she was aware of the warmth of his touch.

He dropped her hand.

"Just a sec," he ordered. "Stay there while I put my bike away."

He went off to another part of the garage, while Marina struggled to put frames of reference together—the boy from ACE . . . Nick Menaker . . . the conversation.

And then she had it.

Of course. Nick was the son the two women had been talking about.

By the time he came back Marina was ready for him. "How come you didn't stay for the party?"

"Wasn't invited," Nick said. "My father doesn't think I particularly showcase the place. And his friends bore me. So I split—by mutual agreement."

Beneath the sullen words Marina sensed bad family relations.

"Too bad. You missed my mother's best chocolate dessert. But there was some left over. Check it out."

"I will." He stood peering down at her, eyes half closed.

"So. Mar-rina." He gave her name the rolling Spanish *r* and made it sound sexy. And then he just stared, not rudely, but so intently that Marina couldn't stand the silence.

"I tried to catch you when you left class today."

"You did? What for?"

"I . . . you left something. I have it."

"What might that be?"

"Two little bells with leather on them."

For the first time he smiled.

"Hey! You found Roxanne's bells and bewits. That's great. I couldn't remember what I did with them."

The semi-darkness gave Marina confidence to move the situation forward. She said teasingly, "I'll give them back to you if you'll tell me who Roxanne is."

Nick Menaker's face was nice when he wasn't trying to play tough guy.

He looked at Marina, raised an eyebrow, and said,

33

"Hint. Rings on her fingers, bells on her toes, she shall have music wherever she goes."

"On whose toes?"

"Roxanne's. She wears those bells on her feet."

That's it! When you hunt with falcons, the bells on their legs tell you where your bird is.

"You're a falconer!" She could picture him with the traditional falconer's glove and a bird perched on his fist.

"Give the girl a great big hand! How'd you know?"

"I go bird-watching a lot. Matter of fact, just today I saw . . ."

She was about to tell Nick Menaker about the platinum peregrine when:

"Is that you out there, Marina?"

It was Isabel calling into the darkness.

"Yes. I'm here."

Her mother's felt presence made her self-conscious.

"I have to be going."

"Yeah. Well—good night," said Nick Menaker. "Uh—see you next Saturday."

"I guess," said Marina, as if her presence on Saturday might be in question. "If I come I'll, uh, bring the bells."

"Okay. Great."

Long pause. Then:

"G'night again."

"Good night."

"Who was that you were talking to out there?" her mother asked on the way home.

"Just some kid from the writing class. Do you have to know everything?"

34

"Sorry," Isabel said. "I did not realize it was a big secret."

"I'm sorry, too." Marina sighed. She just wasn't ready, yet, to tell her mother about Nick Menaker. Because her mother had urged her to meet a boy, maybe? And because this particular boy might not be what Isabel had in mind? Or was it because Nick was a highly disturbing presence— even in the dark.

As between type A and type B, he is a definite B. The kind of boy I'm most afraid of.

Now she had two secrets from Isabel. The stranger and Nick Menaker. Quite a banner day for cover-up. *I'll tell her before we go to bed.*

But she went to sleep without telling Isabel.

CHAPTER

5

LONG AFTERWARD, MARINA WONDERED WHAT would have happened if Isabel hadn't packed the sugar and creamer by mistake.

The next morning her mother said, "Listen, *niña*, I have done a dumb thing. I walked off with the Menakers' silver service by mistake. I found it in with my dishes when we got home last night. I wouldn't want my clients to think I take their *plata*."

"Oh, Mom." Marina laughed at the idea that anyone would think Isabel was a thief.

"Never mind." Isabel was serious. "I called them and told them you would ride over there on your bike and return it."

"Okay."

Isabel looked surprised at Marina's easy agreement, but she said nothing. Nor did she comment when she noticed that Marina brushed and braided her hair carefully before she left.

But she knows something is up. Wise owl. Marina grinned to herself as she tucked the bells and bewits in her pocket.

He probably won't be home, anyway, she said to herself. But her heart beat a little faster when she pedaled up the driveway and saw the motorcycle sitting there.

Nick came to the door, as if he was expecting her.

"Hello there," he said, pretending to be solemn. "Did you come to take back the rest of those cakes? If you did you're out of luck. I had one last night and I am guarding the rest with my life."

Marina laughed and explained her mission.

"Well, in that case you can enter." Nick stepped aside.

Marina suddenly felt shy.

"No, I—I have to go. Here's the stuff." She handed him the box with the silver. "And—oh, I almost forgot." She reached into her pocket and pulled out the bells and bewits.

"Here's your falcon equipment, in case you . . ."

"Well, thanks."

"Yeah, well—I guess I'd better be going."

And then Nick Menaker was saying, "Listen. I'm going into the field tomorrow with Roxanne. It's my last chance before—before she starts to molt. Since you're so interested in birds—ah—maybe you'd like to come."

Match casual with casual. "Why not?"

"Where should I pick you up?"

Decide.

"I'll meet you at Arroyo High. What time?"

37

"Four o'clock. Late afternoon's a good time to go."

"Okay."

Done. A date with Nick the razor cut.

And still she didn't tell Isabel. She merely said, "I won't be home from school until late tomorrow."

Isabel looked surprised.

"Research," Marina muttered.

When she rode her bike into the parking lot the following afternoon, Nick was already there with a big, white English Land Rover. In the back, carefully shielded from the sun, was a perch.

Nick already had the back hatch door open. "Yo. Come see Roxanne," he called, by way of greeting.

Marina peered into the car. There, sitting in regal splendor, was the most beautiful prairie falcon she had ever seen. Roxanne was a pale mottled buff color, about the same size and general shape as the peregrine. That is, what you could see of her. Her face and head were covered by a small hood of maroon leather, topped by a tiny yellow plume. Jesses dangled from her legs, and her bells jangled with each nervous step. In her minuscule battle dress, Roxanne was in a time warp, something straight from the Middle Ages.

"She's lovely."

There was a tan short-haired pointer sitting next to the bird box.

"This is Dusty, who helps us hunt."

"Hi, Dusty." The dog acknowledged the greeting with a thump of his tail.

The falcon danced on her perch impatiently.

"Let's go." Nick picked up Marina's bike and swung it

into the back. "I want to get out there, so we have some time before the sun goes down."

He turned again to the bird. His tone changed, became soft and gentle, as if he were talking to a baby.

"Want to go, don't you, girl? Out where the grouse and the Gambel quail roam. Bet you know it's your last flight before you start molting."

He closed the back gate and they climbed into the Rover.

They headed north, up toward the high desert. Nick supplied no small talk; everything was strictly business.

"She's excited," he offered. "She knows she's going hunting."

"I should think she would. Don't you have to starve her for a few days before the hunt?"

He knit his brows disapprovingly.

"Not starve. Just cut down. So she'll be in hunting shape. 'My falcon now is sharp and passing empty, and till she stoop she must not be full-gorged, for then she never looks upon her lure.' That's Shakespeare. *Taming of the Shrew.*"

So, what we have here is a tough hombre who quotes Shakespeare.

"Then I weigh her to make sure she hasn't lost too much weight or too little. A few ounces in a bird this size can make a difference."

He was like a teacher, explaining his specialty. *Arnheim of the hawks,* Marina thought to herself, smiling at his lecturer tone.

Nick was saying, "Falconry goes way back. Here's a piece of trivia. When Mary Queen of Scots was in the

Tower waiting to be beheaded, her guards would let her out on the parapet every day to fly her merlin."

He paused, as if framing his next statement carefully.

"I'm a general falconer now. That means I can fly a hawk or a longwing, like Roxanne. Apprentice falconers can fly only a kestrel, Harris, red-tail—birds like that. Flying any hawk is fun, but the longwings are the greatest."

In a funny way, falconry seemed the only thing that interested him.

And then they arrived.

It was a more wooded site than the desert Marina was familiar with. Cottonwoods lined the edge of a small stream and oaks and willows made a thicket.

"This is a prairie falcon's natural habitat. Roxanne loves it here."

Nick pulled on his thick falconer's glove.

"Okay, baby, here we go."

Marina watched as Nick reached in and carefully removed Roxanne from the box. He held her gently by the leather jesses and bracelets around her legs.

"She's trained to fly off the fist. The hood is so she won't get nervous with you around. It's a kind of blinders, like those on a horse. I made this one myself. She doesn't mind it. Wait—I'll take it off. Then you can really meet each other."

He lifted the hood. The hawk shook her head, looked around.

"Marina Cassidy," he said formally, "meet Roxanne, my best girl."

"Hello, Roxanne," said Marina softly. "I'm glad to meet you."

The bird turned its head sideways at the sound of the voice, picked up one yellow foot and then the other, all nervous energy and impatience.

"We're about ready to start. I should tell you what's going to happen. I'm about to *cast her off*. She'll fly away, but don't worry. She'll be up there, maybe out of sight, *waiting on*. Then as soon as Dusty finds feathered game, and I flush it, she'll *stoop* for it. She'll spy it from up in the air. I don't have to call her. Then you'll see some action."

"What if Dusty doesn't find anything?"

"Then after a while I'll call her back, and she'll come."

"And if she doesn't?"

"We'll have to follow the sound of her bells. Or we'll go back to the car. She knows the shape of the car. Can you believe it? Sometimes she's waiting there for me."

"Do falconers ever lose a bird?"

"We try not to. But it happens. Worrying about the possibility adds a little extra edge to the enterprise."

Nick tossed Roxanne into the air. She flew in wide circles, gaining altitude until she disappeared. Then he let Dusty out of the car. Dusty scouted the area, his nose to the ground. He entered the longer grass and then he, too, was out of sight. But suddenly they saw the signal flag of his tail up. He had found something in the brush near the creek bed. Dusty was well trained. When he heard Nick's "ho-ho-ho," he stood stock-still. When he sensed Nick coming up in back of him, he stayed low to the ground, his tail and head in a straight line.

Nick and Marina crept forward together. They were almost on top of it before the quarry flushed.

And in that split second, there was Roxanne. This was

41

the moment the falcon had been waiting for. She stooped from her pitch in a dive so steep and swift it sent the wind whistling through her feathers as she plunged by.

Marina held her breath at the sight of the great bird diving, the quail playing the odds, trying with its little brain to decide how to fly to avoid that giant shadow.

The end came with a powerful *Thump!* as the falcon hit its prey in the air with balled feet and raked its body with her talons. A minute later her beak was driving into the bird's neck to sever the spinal cord.

Nick walked over to where the falcon was jealously mantling her prey. He let her have a few bites at the breast. Then, with just a bit of dancing, she allowed him to pick her up with her prey. Nick gently separated the bird from the quail, which he put in a bag. He put Roxanne back on his fist, holding her jesses.

Roxanne wiped her beak on his glove.

"That's called *feaking*," Nick said. "A bird will only clean its beak on you when it's comfortable and feels at home."

Suddenly it was all over. Nick whistled for Dusty, and restored bird and dog to the back of the jeep.

They headed for home.

The adrenalin flow had receded. Marina and Nick were both tired. But that did not entirely explain the strained silence that had begun at the end of the hunt and was growing with every passing minute.

Finally Nick said, "Okay. Out with it. What's the matter? What did I do?"

Marina shivered a little in the evening air.

"You didn't do anything," she murmured.

"I'll bet. All of a sudden, you act as if I had killed somebody. As if you hate me."

He gave a short, mocking laugh. "You don't know me well enough to hate me."

Marina looked across at his hands, tense on the wheel.

"It's just that I—I found it disgusting. The killing, I mean. It wasn't you I hated. I hated myself. Because at the same time I was telling myself how barbaric it was, I was getting a rush. I got a thrill out of the killing."

"We didn't make the kill. The bird did."

"But I enjoyed it. Don't you see? What does that make me?"

"I don't think it makes you anything. If you like to learn about the habits of birds, then this is just one more step. In falconry you get a chance to project what it would be like to put yourself in the bird's place."

"Look. It—it bothered me. But it's none of my business if you like it. I mean, I'm not judging you."

"You sure could have fooled me. But if you think that all falconry is about is the killing, then you didn't get it. You didn't get it at all. There's four thousand years of tradition behind what we did this morning. Do you know how hard I worked to train her to do that and still remain a wild bird? Do you know the trouble it took to"—he hesitated— "to get her, and all the red tape I had to go through to keep her after—" He broke off. "And do you realize how long it took for evolution to make something so perfect?"

"What about the jackrabbit? Isn't it just as perfect?"

"Yeah, As a victim. Rabbits are meat. They're losers."

Now it was Marina's turn to be belligerent.

43

"So that's it. You only like winners, eh?"

"That's right." He was angry now. "I love winners. I love to win. I hate anything I can't do well. That's why I hate the writing class. And it's why I love Roxanne. Because she's a winner. She's a perfect killing machine. What's more, I'm going to buy me another longwing. Something special. I have one on order from a source I know."

Marina immediately thought of the illegal wildlife trade. The smugglers and the story on the radio. This guy is just the type to deal with them. She was angry now. Angry at herself because she had thought this type B might be different. But she'd guessed wrong. *What you see is what you get.*

"I'll tell you what I hate. I hate falconry. And you might as well know it. I'll never do it again."

"Don't worry. You'll never be asked again. Not by me, anyway."

There was nothing to say after that. They sat as far away from each other as possible. Outside, the sun was going down in a dazzling display, but inside the car the mood was dreary.

At last Nick spoke.

"So why did you come then?"

It was a good question.

Marina thought about it for a long while. So long, in fact, that they were in the parking lot of Arroyo High before she answered. As she got out of the Rover she said, almost to herself, "I guess—you could say—I wanted to put myself in the way of experience."

She wasn't sure Nick heard. He leaped out of the car, retrieved her bike, and handed it to her.

"Well, so long," she said. "And thanks, anyway."

Without another word, he climbed into the car and drove away.

And that, thought Marina, *writes finish to that story. The end. Thirty.*

CHAPTER

6

AFTER THE STRANGE RAIN THE LATE SPRING flowers began to bloom. Flashy pink buds appeared on the hedgehog cactus. The prickly pear produced waxy yellow flowers, the saguaro buds opened white. Gaudy annuals began to show themselves—primrose, daisy, purple nama. Bees followed the show, pollen followed bees, snakes mated, birds fed their young. The promise of spring was being kept.

In spite of her bad day with Nick Menaker, Marina looked forward to Saturday and the ACE writing class. She had begun to shape the story of the mysterious peregrine falcons on Montenegro. At first, she unconsciously copied the styles of the nature writers she admired—Sally Carrighar, John McPhee, Annie Dillard. But at last she began to find a voice that was her own. She read the corrected handwritten draft before she left for school. Not too awful.

When she got to class the seat in front of her was empty. It must mean Nick Menaker didn't intend to show. She tried to ignore her letdown feeling. She hadn't realized it, but she had in fact given some thought to how she'd handle seeing Nick Menaker again. *Serves you right*, she told herself. *Bad priorities.*

Just then Nick arrived. He slammed his books down without even glancing in her direction.

What's his problem? Marina wondered. It was almost as if he had been hiding out here in ACE. Here he wasn't Nick Menaker, with a past and a record. He was just another kid, trying to learn how to write. Did he think somehow that meeting her had unmasked him? Or was he still mad because of what she'd said that day he took her out into the field? *What do I care? Spoiled, rich, bad boy. Anyway, am I in this class to come on to a falconer or am I here to learn how to write?*

Turning her mind from Nick, she began to listen to Dr. Arnheim without prejudice. She found that some of his advice made sense. For the rest of the morning it was just between her and the little Chiclet keys.

"The Platinum Peregrine." She entered her story, printed out the first draft, made changes, put them on the screen, lost herself in the work. An hour and a half passed quickly. But when she stopped to rest her eyes she found Nick Menaker staring at her.

"What?" She made it more a flat statement than a question.

"How are you?"

47

"Fine."

"You always so talkative?"

"You always so late with the greetings?"

"Look, I—had some problems this week."

So that was it. Problems. And then the familiar back of the head.

Well, Marina said to herself. *Girl meets boy, girl insults boy, boy has problems. What's next?*

Did the problems have something to do with what she had overheard at the party? Should she keep her mouth shut about knowing? What should she do?

Marina thought of her mother. Isabel would relate, be interested, sympathetic. She would know how to turn a situation like this around. She heard her mother's voice. *Put yourself in the way of experience.*

Carefully, Marina printed out a copy of "The Platinum Peregrine."

She tapped Nick's shoulder.

He turned around.

"Read this," she said, in what she thought was a pleasant but assertive voice.

He hesitated, then took the printout and turned back to his desk.

As soon as he'd finished, he swung around.

"Hey! Is this true? You saw peregrines? An albino?"

His eyes drilled into hers as if they were two pumps reaching into her head to suck information out.

"Where is this place?"

His intensity scared her a little.

"Where did you see peregrines?"

"In—in the desert."

"I know that, but I mean *where?* The exact spot."

Who needs this?

Just then the bell rang.

"Let's finish talking outside."

Bossy, too!

Well. She had certainly gotten Nick Menaker's attention! But now Marina was beginning to feel uncomfortable about what she'd done. She'd enticed Nick Menaker with something that wasn't hers to offer. That was cheap.

He's not interested in me. I'm just a way to the falcons.

They stood on the school steps facing each other.

Nick said, "So. You going to tell, or what?"

"I'm not sure. I hardly know you."

I mean, I know too much about you. Once you were in trouble with the law. You talk about owning falcons, buying them, having contacts.

"For pete's sake. How well do you have to know someone to show him a falcon's nest?"

"First of all, this isn't just any nest. It's an endangered species. They put them in the wild so they'll rebuild populations. But if everybody and his brother knows they're there . . ."

Even she realized how prissy she sounded. She looked away, embarrassed. "There was a news story that . . . some smugglers—maybe falconers—might be taking bird eggs and eyasses out of nests and . . ."

He interrupted, furious.

"That's garbage. You hear? Garbage! Bird smuggling has nothing to do with falconers. Most falconers are on the up-

49

and-up. They police their own ranks. I happen to know!"

"I didn't say *you*. . . . It's just—" What she knew about Nick Menaker hung between them like an invisible fence, forbidding contact.

Nick laid out his credentials.

"Look. I work at a raptor rehab center—uh . . . sometimes. You know, where they get injured birds in shape so they can be hacked back into the wild, and where they raise birds to release into the wild. I have never seen a peregrine falcon nest. The peregrine is the great bird of legend, the first bird to be flown in this country. I would like to see it. It's as simple as that. Yes or no?"

Marina began to feel guilty about her suspicions. Still . . . She decided on a bold move to check him out.

"First take me to the raptor center. I—uh—might like to work there."

"You don't believe my story, do you? Okay, I'll take you over to meet Cheryl."

"Who's Cheryl?"

"She runs the place. If she meets you and decides you're okay, then she might let you clean out the bottoms of the mews and cut up the dead mice."

"Oh, swell. Do you have to pass a test to do that?"

"Not exactly. She'll just see how much you know about raptors."

"You mean to see that I'm not an imposter."

"Something like that." He was suddenly vague. But then he smiled. Nick's teeth gleamed when he smiled.

"She'll see that you're not a bird egg smuggler. Or an international bird thief."

"You don't believe me about that, do you?"

"I do believe you. I heard the story, too. But it has nothing to do with me. Marina Cassidy, read my lips. I am not a falcon smuggler. When do you want to go?"

Marina's chin went up. Adventure. Experience.

"How about right now?"

"You got a deal."

He went to fetch his motorcycle. And left Marina wondering why it was that Nick Menaker could always make her feel strange and unsure. She had started out trying to test him. Now she was going to be tested.

"We can go on my bike."

She looked at the big, fat-tired Harley. "I have my bike, too. The regular kind," she added. "I'll have to bring it home first. My house is about a mile and a half up the hill. That is, if you want to come with me. But maybe it's too far out of your way."

She heard herself giving him handicaps, trying to discourage him.

But Nick Menaker was suddenly endlessly pliant, endlessly accommodating.

"That's okay. You lead. I'll follow." He was already on his motorcycle and revving up.

It was to Isabel's credit that she didn't blink an eye when Marina roared up to the front door in the company of a strange boy on a motorcycle who wore an earring.

"You're home early," was all she said.

Marina's introductions were swift and minimal. No last names.

"Mom, this is Nick. Nick, meet my mom. We're going to a raptor rehab station."

"*Verdad!*" her mother murmured quietly. Marina smiled

to herself. *Verdad* was her mother's Spanish utility word. Depending on how she used it, it could mean "Really?" or "I see" or any number of other appropriate connotations. Marina's guess was that this time it meant, "What's all this?" Marina was not about to explain.

What her mother actually said was, "Hello, Nick. Welcome to Casa Cassidy. You might want a few of those brownies. Take them out of that tray, and I'll refill it when the next batch is done."

"Thanks." Nick helped himself. He took a bite, gasped with pleasure. Then he looked at the brownie in his hand as if it were an unfamiliar object.

"I didn't know mothers made brownies anymore." His tone said he was envious of people who had mothers who did.

Isabel got the hidden message, and fielded it neatly.

"I probably wouldn't make them either, except that it's the way I make my living. You are enjoying one of the fringe benefits of being around someone in the catering business."

Nick frowned. "That's right. I forgot. You catered for my father's party last week."

"Oh?" Her eloquent eyebrows sent new signals to Marina.

Marina shrugged by way of answer. Her shrug pantomimed that he was someone she knew casually and that she had not thought it worth mentioning. Which was not true.

"So can Nick leave his books here?"

"Sure. Just don't leave them on the table. They're liable

to get goo on them. I'm all over the place with this recipe. Put them out in the ramada. They'll be safe there."

While Nick stowed his books, Marina changed into pants and put on her straw hat.

She came back to the kitchen to find Nick and her mother chatting away. Nick had a glass in front of him, and her mother was refilling it with milk.

And another conquest by Isabel Cassidy via the digestive tract.

Nick looked up at Marina. "I like your hat. But you'd better carry it and wear a bike helmet."

"Now that's sensible," Isabel said.

Marina could feel the hot flush burn her cheeks. Already they were in cahoots. *As though I were a baby.*

"Let's go."

"Enjoy." Although Isabel turned back to her baking, Marina felt that her mother was watching every move she made with Nick. Silly, unfair to Isabel maybe, but there it was.

Marina was glad when she and Nick were finally on the bike and away from Casa Cassidy. She held on tight to Nick Menaker. It was by no means unpleasant.

CHAPTER

7

THE THREE R CENTER WAS ALL BUT INVISIBLE from the road. It sat back in a stand of eucalyptus trees, one small green oasis in the sea of cactus and sand. The birds had dictated the choice of this spot. They needed trees, for perch, for cool, for safe cover. But the people, too, derived benefit from the trees. Trees guaranteed shade and cool, and their dropped leaves and blossoms formed the soft path on which Marina and Nick now walked.

"So she owns all this, Cheryl what's her name?"

"Harper. Yeah. She inherited it or something."

"She married?"

"I think she had a husband for a while. If that's relevant."

Marina pulled a leaf from a eucalyptus, rubbed it between her fingers, and inhaled the familiar, pleasant smell of the oil.

"How old a woman is she?"

"I'd guess about thirty-five."

Hmm.

They had reached the house now, and Nick was steering her around to the back.

"She'll be outside at the mews," he explained.

The house was large and rambling. It had a butterfly roof that hung out on either side of the main part of the house like a pair of huge wings. The mews, where the raptors were kept, were underneath. There were eight of them, four on each side. Each was about twelve feet high, eight feet wide, large enough for a person to stand and walk around in. More importantly, they were large enough for birds to fly in. They were made of cinder block sunk halfway into small hillocks on either side of the path which led to the house. The fronts were made of wire, set in front of bars of plastic pipe designed to contain the birds but separate them from the wire that was so dangerous to their feathers and talons. Because of the overhang and the clever construction, the avian boarders got light and air but were buffered against rain, sandstorms, or night cold. But the roof also had an oddly symbolic effect. House and mews together looked like a giant bird mantling— spreading its wings over what was beneath, as if to protect the contents from prying eyes.

Just then the door to one of the mews opened.

"And there she is now!" Nick announced, his voice like a fanfare.

A tall, pretty, red-haired woman in a short skirt and high boots was striding toward them. Cheryl Harper was defi-

nitely a presence. Everything about her spelled drama—
the mop of hair, the outsize Indian jewelry, the slash of red
lipstick. She waved her hand in a gesture of greeting, and
Marina noticed another riveting detail. Cheryl Harper's
nails were extraordinarily long—and curved like talons.
But instead of being pale yellow, like a raptor's, they were
deep blood red—exclamation marks at the ends of her long
white fingers.

"How you doing?" she called huskily. But her eyes were
on Marina, asking Nick silently, *Who is this?*

Nick's voice was carefully casual.

"Cheryl, this is Marina Cassidy. She's in that writing
class I told you about. She's a birder, and—um—she
wanted to see the birds and maybe ask you about working
with raptors."

"Ah-huh!" She turned toward Marina and subjected her
to long and acute surveillance. Cheryl's eyes managed to
suggest a hawk. But it wasn't only the eyes. Marina wondered if Nick had noticed that the woman who worked
with hawks seemed to have taken on some of their charac-
teristics. There was hawk mimicry in the turn of her head,
the sideways glance, even in the alert tension of her body
language. As if she were ready to fly off. Or to pounce?
The question was—why was Cheryl Harper so tense?

"Nice to meet you, Marina," Cheryl finally said in a
voice that reserved judgment. She turned to Nick. "May I
talk to you for a minute?"

They stepped away from Marina. Cheryl began to murmur an urgent aside. Marina stood rooted to the spot,
uncomfortable but curious. She caught only a few words.

56

"I'm still furious—that little stunt you pulled—Roxanne —get me into trouble."

That was all. Suddenly Cheryl's voice changed; she became brisk and businesslike.

"Update on Harriet. I think her eggs will start to pip about Monday. You can hear the chicks inside them now."

"That's terrific."

She turned to Marina and said, in a slightly friendlier tone, "Harriet and Harry, our Harris hawks, are brooding four eggs. If all goes well, we'll have four young hawks in a week or so."

"No kidding!"

But Marina's head was with the whispered conversation. *What does Roxanne have to do with Cheryl? And why does Nick look like a naughty child?*

Nick was making rapid small talk, as if to cover up.

"Maybe you'll get to see them. Maybe."

Teasing. But all the while his eyes were on Cheryl. It was as if he needed something from her, some approval or—stories she'd heard about boys and older women ran through Marina's mind. She couldn't enter into the animated conversation Nick and Cheryl were having with their eyes. She studied Cheryl. You had to admit, there was something exotic about Cheryl Harper's style. She thought of her mother. Isabel was exotic, too, in a different way.

Exotic probably came from experience. *Wherever it comes from, I want it.*

Cheryl turned to Marina.

"That screaming you hear is some of the patients who

57

are feeling better hollering for their lunch. I'm just about to feed them. Would you like to watch?"

"I really would."

"Come along then. Nicky, you go get the food while I show Marina around."

Nicky?

Without another word, Nick turned and went to do Cheryl's bidding.

As she walked toward the supply shed, she tried to forget about Nick and listen to what Cheryl was saying.

"We get birds here from all over Arizona. We're licensed for both raptor rehab and for restoration of raptor populations. That means we can take in owls, hawks, falcons, or eagles, and do captive breeding. Three R—raptor rehab and restoration. Get it? Pretty much everyone finds us sooner or later." Then she added, "Sometimes that's good. Sometimes it's not so great."

She paused at the first mew.

"We'll feed Damon first. Damon's a goshawk. Got him through a phone call from someone east of here. He'd been shot by someone who took a dim view of his chasing after the chickens. We're imping him. That means substituting a few feathers. We graft them on with bamboo."

Nick joined them, carrying a metal cookie sheet. Tiny dead chicks lay on it in neat rows.

"Have an hors d'oeuvre," he said, pretending to pass the tray to Marina and Cheryl. And then, in a perfect imitation of Isabel, he said, "Help yourself from this tray. I'll refill it when I bake the next batch."

Marina burst out laughing.

Cheryl Harper ignored the repartee. "We're feeding them vitamin A this morning."

In answer to Marina's questioning look she said, "Feeding a hawk a chick is like giving it a vitamin pill. But you can't give them only chicks. They'd eat a variety of things in the wild."

Marina watched the red nails curl around a dead chick.

"Damon was pretty sick when we got him. Half dead, matter of fact. We fed him only fluids for a while, and it was touch and go. But now he's all healed and eating well. Won't be long before we can release him."

"Okay. Here we go. Nick, you stay out. We'll go in, give him the food, and leave. I don't want to hang around and neither should you. He's a wild bird going back to the wild. There's no reason for him to get too used to people."

They entered the mew. A huge gray and brown goshawk sat on its perch. Cheryl put the food on a stand nearby. In a flash the bird was on the chick and eating. But it was not so concentrated on the task that it did not see Marina. Without stopping its feeding, it turned its fierce eye on her. Its hackles stood up and made a crown on its gray head. It turned its back, ostentatiously, and mantled the food. It was a formidable sight—the great hawk tearing at the flesh and menacing a possible enemy at the same time.

They moved along the mews from bird to bird. Cheryl kept up an animated conversation. Marina was impressed with the fact that she knew her stuff. And she sure was putting on a show. Except that there was that tension in her voice, in the way she moved. But maybe she was always like that.

"This great horned owl is a permanent guest. Her wing was wrecked and it will never heal enough so she can fly. Name's Florence and she'd eat one of the hawks if she had half a chance."

"And here's Ramon." Marina looked in on a handsome young Harris hawk eating chicken on a wooden platform.

"We got this guy as an eyass. He was electrocuted by a wire. He was so sick it has taken us a full year to get him back on his feet. During that time he got pretty used to us—what we call *habituated*. Now we're hacking him back to his wild state. That's why he's eating on that platform. After a while we'll put it outside. Then gradually we'll train him to find food on his own, and he'll stop coming to the platform. Then he'll be ready to be released."

Marina was remembering the hunt.

"An awful lot of raptor behavior has to do with eating, doesn't it?"

"You bet," said Cheryl. "Eating is what these guys are all about. They're predators, designed for the hunt. They've evolved into the most incredibly efficient machines for killing. No energy wasted, nothing killed for sport. It's beautiful to watch."

She gazed into the distance, as though she were seeing a hawk hunting in her mind's eye.

Nick gave Marina an I-told-you-so look.

"Are you a falconer, too?" Marina asked.

"Yes, when I have the time. But mainly I'm busy saving birds. I don't have time to fly them. I leave that to—other people."

Marina nodded. "Like Nick."

"Yeah, well—"

Nick's eyes pleaded with Cheryl about something.

Abruptly, she changed the subject.

"Which reminds me." She turned to Nick. "Let's go up to the house. I need to talk to you."

"Sure."

She scrutinized Marina again. She seemed to make up her mind about something.

She looked at Nick. "I hope to heaven you have truly turned over a new leaf, boy-o. Because this is important, Nick. Very important."

Nick's whole attitude toward Cheryl seemed to change. In a voice almost humble, he said, "Hey, Cheryl, come on. You know that's over."

What's over? Portrait shooting? Falcon stealing? What?

But before she had answered that question, another one surfaced. As they walked, Cheryl began to talk, quickly, in a low, husky voice.

"There's a ring of wild bird smugglers operating in this area."

Nick nodded. And Marina said, "I know. I heard about it on the radio."

"Okay then," Cheryl went on. "They're mainly after longwings. Falcons. They try to get them across the border. From there they're shipped to Europe and the Middle East, where they're bought by wealthy falconers who don't care how they spend their money. Do you believe a healthy gyrfalcon can go for as much as a hundred thousand dollars? Greed makes everyone get big eyes and then things get rough."

Marina couldn't help interrupting.

"But what does that have to do with us? Gyrfalcons are arctic birds. There are no gyrs here in Arizona."

"I know that. But they're bringing them from Canada and sending them across the border down here."

"How do they get them across the border?"

"With great inventiveness! They just caught a couple running falcon eggs across the border. They had painted them to look like those Polish Easter eggs!"

She paused. "Now something weird is happening. I think the Feds are trying to figure out how they can crack the ring from inside. They've been here all day, looking over my rehab license, my breeding licenses, and every other blasted record I have. Incidentally, they're asking me about everyone who works here or comes here. I had to give them your name, Nick. I wanted to call you before they came by, but I didn't have a chance."

Nick looked pale, but he came on tough.

"I'm not worried."

"Well, you should be." There was a bitter note in Cheryl's voice. "The government can be pretty unreasonable sometimes. They can cast a pretty wide net, and sometimes little fish get caught in it. Especially when they have a previous . . ."

"Never mind." Nick cut her off. "What about the people who were caught? Can't they get information from them?"

"They're not in any shape to talk right now. And when they do, they're not going to give the names of the big guys behind this. They'll implicate some small breeder or falconer. The Feds will try to get to the big guns through rollovers. You know, the little fry implicate the bigger ones and so on up the line. To the top, if they're lucky." Her tone turned bitter.

"Y'know, it's ironic. We finally get the government interested in saving endangered species. Then they come along, and the very legislation that we helped set up, they turn against us. They won't rest now. Every raptor breeder, every rehab center, every little *schnook* who flies a falcon or watches birds is going to be suspect. You know what they'll do? They'll infiltrate. You won't know who's your friend and who's your enemy. They'll entrap, they'll tempt. It'll be a real *sting*. Wait, you'll see. Before they're through, an awful lot of birds will die. And a lot of falconers will get hurt."

Now Cheryl seemed to be weighing something.

Finally she said, "You know, Nick, it might be better if you didn't hang out here for a while. I—well, there's no reason for you to get involved."

She turned to Marina.

"That goes for you, too. I'd like to have you help me, but maybe we'd better wait till this thing blows over."

"But I want to be involved," Marina heard herself saying.

"I don't!" Nick said. "I'm going to make myself scarce. Keep my nose clean."

Cheryl nodded approvingly.

"What about feeding the birds?" Marina begged. "I could do that, anyway. Take a little of the work off your hands."

And this is a place where things are happening.

Marina could feel Cheryl's hesitation.

At last she said, "Well—okay. I sure could use some-body, especially when the Harris hawks start hatching. But I don't think Nick should be here. We're in for a real"— she paused —"bad time. Nick's vulnerable."

And then she said something that made Marina's skin prickle.

"They think the smugglers have established a local base. In other words, they're scouting the birds from Serenity. That has to mean only one thing. *Peregrines*. It's illegal to fly wild ones or take them from the wild for any reason, as you know. We'll have to really watch things. If anyone should get wind of breeding pairs or nestlings in the wild . . ."

Marina felt an urgent pressure on her arm. Nick was sig-naling clearly: *Don't say anything.*

They left shortly afterward.

"Why didn't you want me to tell Cheryl?"

"Because I know Cheryl. She'll pick your brains the way Roxanne pieces on a quail. I just think—the fewer people know the better. Why take any chances?"

That's what I think. So why am I taking you there, Nick Menaker?

"Speaking of chances, what was that little aside about something you did illegally?"

"I'll explain—after our trip to the mountain."

Marina let it go. But she couldn't help wondering why she kept getting only part of the story.

64

CHAPTER

8

THE NEXT AFTERNOON NICK MENAKER CALLED to ask when they could go to see the peregrine nest.

No. I need time to sort out Cheryl Harper, the Three R, bird smuggling.

"I have to help my mother today," she said.

Isabel rolled her eyes skyward and made faces.

"How about tomorrow?"

Marina made up another excuse.

But Nick wouldn't take no for an answer. He pursued the subject. "I'm holding you to your promise," he told her. "What do you say?"

Finally she agreed to go on the following day—Tuesday. Isabel pretended her attention was all on some little cream puffs she was making, but Marina knew she was listening. The Isabel quiz wasn't long in coming.

"So what kind of boy is this Nick Menaker?"

"Surly."

"Ah! Surly, and with an earring, and drives a motorbike. That begins to form a picture."

"It sure does. Not a pretty one either. I'd like to know where the surliness comes from."

"You will, in time." Isabel licked a bit of cream from her finger. "You are a born prober, I think. You want to find out how everything works, even people. Anyway, he seems like a nice boy inside the rough-tough package, don't you think?" And then she added, with a sly smile, "Anyone who loves chocolate brownies can't be all bad."

Isabel left the room. Marina looked after her, thinking.

Isabel likes Nick. Isabel likes everybody.

But Isabel didn't know about that conversation at the party between the two women. Or what Cheryl had said about something Nick had done. Cheryl didn't want him around her rehab station. Why? What had Nick meant about keeping his nose clean?

The second phone call came while Isabel was away.

"Is this Marina Cassidy?"

"Yes, it is."

"We understand that you're a birder. We're in the process of preparing a new Southwestern bird atlas, and we've started a kind of hotline. People phone in and report the birds they see and where they see them. And the person who sees the rarest birds gets a prize at the end of the year."

The caller's voice went up slightly at the end of her spiel, as if there was a built-in question.

Marina asked how they had gotten her name.

66

"Oh, we know you're a member of Audubon," the caller said smoothly.

That sounded legitimate. Marina felt slightly flattered to have been chosen.

"Tell me what I have to do."

"All you have to do is let us know whenever you see unusual birds. Particularly hawks and falcons."

Wait a minute.

She felt the faint stirring of suspicion, but decided to play along.

"What do I do if I see something?"

"We'll call you every week to pick up your data."

Hmm. Don't call us, we'll call you.

"What's the prize if I see a rare species?"

"We'll pay one hundred and fifty dollars for a positive identification of a rare hawk or falcon, if you can give an exact place of the sighting."

Marina knew before she hung up that it was a phony call. *Whoever that was must think I was born last week.* She was pleased at her own perception. Still, the call made her nervous. There was someone out there who knew her, knew where to reach her, and knew of her interest in birds! She wondered whether she should report the call. To Cheryl Harper, for instance. But that idea led to another. Maybe Cheryl was involved in the smuggling. Maybe that was why the government was so busy investigating Three R. On the other hand, Cheryl had told her about the Feds. She wouldn't have done that if she had something to hide. And she certainly seemed to care deeply about birds.

Her mind leaped to another unpleasant possibility.

Maybe Nick was the leak. Maybe he'd already told someone about the peregrine! But why? Was it because he was
helping the investigation or because he was part of the
gang being investigated? Marina was beginning to see the
built-in problem that exists with a sting. It's hard to tell the
sting-er from the sting-ee!

The third phone call was from Cheryl Harper.

"I wanted to tell you that Harry and Harriet's offspring
—you remember, the Harris hawks—have been peeping
in the eggs for a couple of days now. The first one started
to pip—break out—this afternoon. Gee. Everything happens at once. It's liable to take awhile. And you said you
wanted to be involved and help out. So I thought maybe, if
you could—"

Cheryl sounded so tense and worried over the hawks
that Marina immediately dismissed the thought that she
was involved in illegal bird traffic.

"I'll be right over."

She would have been out the door except for Cheryl's
speedy, "No. Wait a sec. Make it an hour or so. By that
time I'll be looking for someone to spell me. And—look,
Marina. Do me a favor. I don't know quite how to say this,
but—don't tell Nick you're coming. What he doesn't know
won't hurt him. I don't want him around here if—well,
just don't. Okay?"

"Sure. I guess."

*He doesn't trust her and she doesn't trust him. Or
they're trying to protect each other. Or something.*

"How's seven o'clock?"

"Sounds good." She hung up.

Just then Isabel came back. She wanted to know what the phone call was about.

"Nothing much." Marina tried to sound casual. "It was that woman from the rehab center. The one I told you about, remember? She just wanted to tell me that some Harris hawks are almost ready to hatch. She wants me to come over."

"Tell me, what are this Cheryl and her bird sanctuary like?"

"They're the answer to your suggestion about putting myself in the way of experience."

"*Verdad!* I thought Nick Menaker was the answer to that."

"Don't be funny, *Madre*. That place just looks like the setting for a story. I could never make up a place like that. And what is going on there, I mean, what I think may be going on there—it's a fantastic plot. Old Arnheim will be pleased! You will be pleased!"

"Okay, I'm pleased. Now tell me the facts."

"The facts are, somehow Cheryl is involved with that bird scam. Someone is trying to buy birds from her and the government is investigating her or—she's involved in some way. It's exciting."

"Mmm." Isabel didn't look excited; she looked worried.

"Now remember. I don't want you riding home in the dark," she warned. "If it gets late, call me, and I'll come get you."

"Hey, Ma, you're getting to be a real worry wart. *No problema.* I'll be okay."

But Isabel was adamant.

69

"Don't 'no problema' me. I hear what's going on around here. Suddenly everyone in Serenity is talking about bird smugglers and border crossings and investigations. There is a *problema*. So promise."

"Okay. I promise."

"Good."

Marina found Cheryl at the mews, looking worried.

"I'm glad you're here," she said. "Something's wrong. It's taking too long this time. And Harriet is acting funny. She actually called me. I heard her way up in the house. They'll do that, you know. I think the chick is stuck in the shell. I'm going in there. You'd better come, too. I'll want you to lift the other eggs out of the way while Harriet and I work on Chicken Little."

"Okay. Sure. But won't they be afraid of a stranger?"

"Not if you're with *me*. They trust me. Heck, I'm practically the godmother of those eggs!"

The expectant parents hunched on branches in the back of the mew, stretching their talons. They kept up a stream of nasal nattering.

"Before you go in, I should give you a little background on these two," Cheryl said. "First of all, Harris hawks mate for life. And they live in family groups in the wild. I'm sure you've seen them nesting in a cactus."

Marina nodded.

"The body of this nest is made of sticks, and it sits on an old wine cask. My contribution. Actually, I brought the sticks, but Harry made the final selections. He checked out each one. He'd hold it in his talons, look it over, then either drop it on the floor or put it on the nest. Believe me, many were brought but few were chosen!"

"This is their second brood. For three days they've been talking like this, ever since the first sounds started coming from the eggs. I figure they're calling to the chicks—encouraging them to come out."

They entered the mew and approached the nervous birds. As soon as Cheryl was able to get a good look at the egg, she saw what had happened. Somehow the baby bird's wing was pinned inside the egg. Struggle as it would, it could not get out. The mother was trying to help, but in her frantic pecking she was coming perilously close to the little hawk's eyes. As for the baby hawk, it was getting exhausted.

Cheryl said, "I'm going to have to chip away at this shell." She moved as she spoke. "Careful," she advised herself. "No," she told Harriet gently, as the bird tried once again to peck the baby bird free.

Marina was amazed. The bird stopped pecking and moved away. Could she have understood? Cheryl began to delicately break away tiny pieces of shell. The membrane had to remain undisturbed, so the chick wouldn't dry out before it emerged.

It was slow work. The parent birds kept up a steady, grating squawking, and the baby bird peeped pathetically in answer.

"The only thing more nerve-racking than that peeping would be if it stopped," Marina said.

Time dragged by. Cheryl talked as she worked, while Marina did what she could to be an extra pair of hands.

"There are two schools of thought about this hatching business. Some breeders say humans shouldn't intervene the way I'm doing. You know, let 'em hatch by themselves or not at all. But I think otherwise. Every egg counts in my book. I've even been known to patch cracked eggs with Elmer's glue. It works fine."

Marina's back began to protest the enforced hunched position. But finally Cheryl said quietly, "Okay. Done." At the same moment, the female gave a scream of triumph. The hawk chick was out of its shell, a little the worse for wear but otherwise unharmed.

"How about calling it Harrison?" Marina whispered, looking down at the wet blob with the oversize feet. "You know, son of Harris?"

Cheryl smiled tiredly. "Good idea. Unless she's Harris-daughter, and I'm too tired right now to check."

Cheryl and Marina left the Harris family.

"Let's go in and have a cold drink," Cheryl said.

"Okay. And I'd better call my mother. What time is it, anyway?"

Cheryl looked at her watch.

"Good Lord! It's midnight. I think you'd better stay over. Phone's there. Give your mom a ring and ask her."

Marina called Isabel, who agreed that it was too late to think about coming home.

"You can sleep in that little room over there," Cheryl said to Marina, waving a hand toward a closed door. "The bed's made up. Get up whenever you want tomorrow. Help yourself to breakfast if I'm gone. There are plenty of eggs." She made a face. "If you still eat eggs, after this evening." She shook her head. "Egg-wise, I'd say this has been quite a week. Some folks saving them, and some folks smuggling them."

Marina nodded sleepily. "That reminds me. Have they found out anything more about those painted eggs, or about the smugglers?"

"Not that I know of. The two people they picked up are from Germany, but the Feds don't think they're the ringleaders."

"Did they ever find out what kind of eggs they were?"

"Yes. They were peregrine eggs."

Marina's heart lurched.

"From where?"

"Who knows? Those folks ain't telling. Most likely they bought them illegally from someone. An individual. Or a dishonest raptor breeding project. There aren't that many wild eyries around here anymore."

Maybe it was fatigue that caused Marina to forget Nick's admonition.

"I saw one," she blurted.

And she proceeded to tell Cheryl about the peregrines. At first Marina sensed that Cheryl didn't believe her, but after she filled in the details, Cheryl asked, "When? When did you first see them?"

"About two weeks ago. They're probably hatched out now. That is, if . . . There were four eggs in the nest when I saw it last week."

"That was probably the full brood. Wasn't the eyrie high up? How in the world did you get to see them?"

"With great difficulty." Marina grinned as she described her climb and the tiercel's attack on her.

"Good!" Cheryl was grim. "Let's hope no one else was able to get past him. Those eyasses are doubly valuable because of the female's coloring. Good Lord. They might even try to take her!"

A few seconds later Cheryl asked, almost too casually, "Where did you say the place was?"

Marina hesitated. *I didn't say.* But then she thought, *What's the matter with me? This is Cheryl Harper. I just helped her save a baby bird. She can be trusted.*

And so Marina sleepily drew a crude map on a piece of paper towel, and showed Cheryl how to get to Montenegro. When she had finished, she said, "I'm going to go back there day after tomorrow. I mean tomorrow. I need to see if the eggs are still there."

But she didn't tell Cheryl that Nick wanted to go with her.

"I'm wiped. Going to hit the sack. Good night, Cheryl. And listen, if I don't see you in the morning, call me when Mama Harriet's other two are out."

"Yeah. I'll call you to come over and skin some mice and bone them. Papa doesn't like that job. Refused to do it last time, so you or I will have to prepare the 'baby food.' "

"My pleasure. Anything for a hawk friend."

Cheryl still sat at the table, staring gloomily into space.

"Aren't you going to go to bed?" Marina asked.

Cheryl nodded, but didn't make a move to get up. At last she said, "I'll tell you one thing. I hate the idea of someone taking all those rare birds and shipping them to Lord knows where and maybe killing them because they don't give them the proper care. I'd do almost anything to help get this business cleared up." She paused, then added, "Almost anything. But I don't like shenanigans."

What shenanigans?

Marina slept well. It was nine o'clock when she was fully awake. She padded in to the kitchen. No signs of life. Cheryl was probably already out at the mews, feeding her rehabs and checking Dad and Mom Harris and the baby. She helped herself to a bagel and some orange juice and sat down at the kitchen table.

The man entered the kitchen quietly. He stood, perfectly poised, hairy legs sticking out from beneath a short terry robe, face devoid of surprise. He waited for her to say something. When she didn't, he came toward her with his hand out.

"Sam Spenser." Then, as if that explained everything, he proceeded to investigate the contents of Cheryl's refrigerator in a way that said he'd done it before.

Marina took a swallow of orange juice.

"Marina Cassidy. I stayed overnight."

"Uh-huh. Well, don't let me interrupt your breakfast."

He knew. He knew who she was and that she had stayed over.

He took out fruit and yogurt, found a box of cereal on a shelf. Then he sat down across from her.

"I'm an old friend of Cheryl's," he said. "I was passing through, so I said I'd stay awhile and help out. You know, with the breeding and all."

So then why did Cheryl need me?

Just then, Marina glanced at the doorway. There was Cheryl, standing with a cup of coffee in her hand. She was studying the cup as if it held her fortune.

"Yah," she said finally. "I was *sooo* surprised to see old Sammy."

She wasn't. I don't believe it. Who is Sam Spenser? Is he

her lover? And if he is, why didn't she say so? What am I, two years old?

Marina studied Sam Spenser's face. The man was attractive in a rumpled, slightly shabby way. His eyes were tired and cynical; his face showed faint scars of old acne. But, like a dueling scar, the slight disfigurement enhanced his looks, made him memorable. Memorable, yes. He was memorable. Marina had seen this barrel-chested gent before.

Much later that day, after she was home, she remembered. She was quite sure Sam Spenser was the man she had seen through her binoculars that day on the mountain.

CHAPTER

9

ON TUESDAY MORNING THE SUN WAS BLOOD red, promising a scorching day in Serenity. Marina heard Nick before she saw him. She made a mental note to write about the fact that sounds call up people. Nick Menaker's sound was a motorcycle.

And now here he was, wearing a thin Arab turban that fell to his shoulders in soft patterned blue folds.

He bowed in a mock salaam to Isabel. With his blond head covered, the tan, and the sunglasses, Nick Menaker looked as though he'd stepped out of *Lawrence of Arabia*.

He seemed a different Nick in other ways as well. Today he was warm, smiling, considerate.

Now he turned to Marina.

"It's going to be hot out there. I brought one for you,

too." He handed her a soft square of fabric patterned in red.

"It's called a *keffia*," he said. "I brought them back from one of my trips to the Middle East."

The Middle East? One of his trips? The remark set off a chain reaction. Wasn't the Middle East where the stolen falcons ended up? And why was Nick Menaker commuting back and forth to that particular spot on the globe? The little aside was enough to refuel her suspicions.

"Thanks. I'll wear my hat."

"Sure. Wear your hat on top of it. It'll look great. Here. Wait. I'll fix it for you."

With Isabel watching, Nick deftly adjusted the keffia on her head and then put the hat on top of it.

"Now come, little one. Mount my steed and I shall spirit you away into the sunset. Er—make that motorcycle and sunrise."

Isabel giggled, but all Marina said was, "Leave your bike here. You'll chew up the whole desert riding that thing where we're going. We'll walk in. Here's the water jug. We should have started earlier. We'll bake out there now."

For a moment, Nick looked dismayed—but he rallied and said jauntily, "Hey! I don't care how we travel as long as we get there."

They followed the trail that Marina had taken the previous week. But today it felt different—hotter and more hostile. The smell of the creosote bushes was sharp and acrid, unpleasant to the nostrils. The jumping cholla seemed to have grown up overnight; its needle-sharp arms were everywhere, like barbed wire strung through a no-man's-land. And the heat was pitiless, a shimmering haze through which they walked, their shadows trailing like silent ghosts.

Marina knew that at least part of her discomfort was her worry that she had already said too much about the birds and their young. Cheryl knew about them and soon Nick would know, too. She should have kept her mouth shut.

When they saw the tiny blue bird impaled on the cactus spike, it seemed somehow to fit Marina's mood.

Nick made a face when she pointed it out to him.

"That's disgusting. How'd it get there?"

"Loggerhead shrike must have stashed it. They're predatory birds. They attack small songbirds like this bluebird, then hang them to hold them for a later meal. Like on a butcher's meat rack."

They walked past it in silence.

Playing to the Isabel gallery seemed to have exhausted Nick's store of conversation. Finally, as much to break the silence as anything, Marina took on the role of tour guide. As they followed the dry arroyo, she showed Nick her favorite clumps of paloverdes. She named the cacti. She took him off the trail to show him the mound festooned with shiny objects that was a pack rat midden.

They had gone about a mile when Nick suddenly said, "Hold it a sec." He stopped to pick up a sturdy branch of cottonwood. Marina watched as he cut it with his pocket knife and made a makeshift walking stick.

Marina realized guiltily that the leg he favored was

really bothering him. She should have thought about that when she so summarily dismissed going on the motorcycle.

But the stick seemed to lend Nick support. And for more than just his leg. For the first time, he began to open up about himself. Marina found out that he had spent a year at the state university taking business administration courses, had hated it, had flunked out, and for this year was "hanging out" at home.

"I'm supposed to be finding myself," he said, with a trace of a smile. "That's why I took the writing course. But I'm rotten at that, too, and I don't get better. I guess I'm looking for something I don't stink at."

Now there was a frank statement.

She probed to get more—a clearer picture of the real Nick Menaker.

"What about falconry? You're good at that. Doesn't that satisfy you?"

"In a way it does. But you can't make a career out of falconry. Or so my esteemed father informs me. Sure would be nice, though. Getting paid for doing what you enjoy."

He seemed to have forgotten that Marina hated falconry. His voice grew animated as he started to talk about the lure of the ancient sport.

"Falconry's great because it's not about owning something. The thing is, you never make a pet of the bird. The bird is on its own, doing what it does naturally. You just help it develop its skill even further. It's a partnership. After you've trained her to the fist and entered her to quarry—that first time you hood her to take her to the

80

field—when your bird *waits on* up in the clouds some-place—you're right there in the air with her. And then you watch that swift kill—"

"Do me a favor. Skip the killing part."

"Oh, yeah. I forgot." But instead of arguing, Nick oblig-ingly changed course.

"And when you don't want to keep a falcon anymore, you can hack it back to the wild, if you do it right. By the way, did you know that in medieval times couples were married with their falcons on their fists? The bride and groom hunted as part of the honeymoon."

Abruptly he changed the subject.

"So where is *your* father, Marina? Are your folks divorced, too?"

"No, my father's dead."

"Oops. Sorry."

"It's okay. I don't mind talking about it. He died of a heart attack when I was a kid. Will was a painter. First-generation Irish Expressionist, he called himself. I'll show you some of his paintings sometime, if you like."

Nick said quietly, "I would like."

He didn't say anything for a while. And then, "So you're Spanish-Irish? Where'd you get the name Marina? Did you know that's the name of an Aztec princess?"

"I knew it. But how did you know?"

"Listen, I may look like a bike freak, but I'm really a hot dog in history."

Curiouser and curiouser.

Nick studied her seriously.

"You *look* a little like an Aztec princess, with that inky

hair and those cheekbones. How does the Irish part show up?"

"Fair skin. Sunburn. More important, I'm hoping it'll make me a great writer. You know. O'Casey, Joyce, Yeats."

"Sounds like a law firm."

Marina laughed. "That's enough oral history of the Cassidys for one day. How about your family tree?"

She looked full at him and was surprised that he avoided her eyes.

"Nothing special," he murmured, as if talking to the sand at his feet. "Pure WASP. Family's been here for generations. They all went to good Eastern colleges and made big bucks in banking. My father's some kind of foreign investment honcho. My mother—"

He stopped abruptly, took a breath, and said, "My mother ran off with a young guy, not much older than me."

Marina felt he was waiting for her to say something.

"There's a lot of that around," she murmured.

Nick stopped talking. Marina hated not to hear the end of the story. She probed the tender area carefully.

"So how are things now? Do you see your mother?"

"Not too often. She gives me a pain in the—well, head actually. I always get a migraine after I see her. And my father—he has pretty set ideas about what I should do and what I should be. Never satisfied. When I took the writing class, I thought he would approve. So then he says on the phone he thinks it's a stupid idea."

"Is that why you came to school last week looking so mad?"

"No. That was because I had a fight with Cheryl. About

82

taking Roxanne out hunting. It's—kind of complicated."
He sighed. "Right now, I'm sort of on probation and
I'm—grounded as a falconer. I'm not allowed to keep Rox-
anne, so Cheryl's taking care of her for me and—"

"So that's what you two were talking about the other
day, isn't it?"

Nick refused to meet her eyes. Instead he looked off
into the distance, where the mountains were just visible
through a shimmering haze.

"Hey! Is that it? Your famous Montenegro? Looks like
every other cliff to me. You sure that's the one?"

"Positive."

As they moved closer, he looked more and more worried.

"Is that where it is? Way up there?"

"Yeah. *Way* up. You know, peregrines always make their
nests high up on cliffs. It's hard to get to, all right. But—"
She saw the look on his face. "Anything wrong?"

"I didn't realize it was so steep. I wonder if I can do it
with this foot."

"I noticed you limping. What's wrong with it, anyway?"

"I—uh—smashed it. Doesn't work all that well yet."

"How'd you do it?"

"It's a long story. But the point is, I'm not sure I can
make it up that mountain."

"I'll give you a hand. Don't worry, I know the way and
there are some good footholds. You can do it."

Nick looked at her with something unreadable in his
face.

"Don't be too sure. The foot isn't mine."

Artificial foot. So that's what those expensive Frye boots are hiding.

"When did it happen?"

"When I was eighteen. Right after the divorce. Call it an attention-getting device. I got into a little—well—trouble. I was on the bike trying to—making my getaway, as they say in the novels, when I crossed paths with a new driver. It was at night, he zigged when he should have zagged, and—there you are. I get a mashed foot and a broken leg, the other kid gets a lifelong guilt complex. Two young lives affected, as the judge said."

He gave a short, barking laugh.

"So how come you still ride the motorcycle? Isn't that asking for it?"

"You have to climb back on the horse. Besides, I'm betting on the law of averages. I've had mine."

"Well, that's pretty silly." Marina felt angry and confused by her own complex emotions over the motorcycle story.

She exploded.

"You know, Nick Menaker, you keep feeding me little pieces, like a puzzle. But you never tell me the whole story. So I can't be truly comfortable with you. And I'm sick of being under a strain. Are we going to trust each other or not?"

She stood there in the heat, glaring at him.

Nick hesitated. Finally he nodded.

"Okay. You asked for it. Better sit down for this one."

Nick reached for her hand, as if he needed something to hold onto as he talked. And so at last, in the heat of a May morning, Marina heard Nick Menaker's story.

CHAPTER

10

"AFTER MY MOTHER LEFT WITH THAT GUY, I just—I don't know. I guess I was mad at the world. I wanted to kill. I got heavily into hunting. I'd go out into the desert and pop off rabbits, birds, anything that moved. I was your stereotypical plinker—the kind that gives even the National Rifle Association a headache. I can't explain it." He stopped and took a breath. "I took some eyasses out of nests to sell to falconers. I even trapped some passage birds and haggards—mature birds. Not for the money. Just for the hell of it."

Marina tried not to let her expression show how shocked she was. She waiting for him to go on.

"So then one day I saw this eagle. I didn't really think about it much. I just aimed and shot it. Somebody saw me and reported it. I tried to get away, but they caught me.

That was when I hurt the foot. After I recovered, there was a trial. The fine was stiff—five thousand bucks. But the judge realized that wouldn't mean all that much to a Menaker. So he sentenced me to a year of community service, at Cheryl Harper's place."

"So that's how you met Cheryl?"

"Yeah. She's been great. She turned me around in my attitudes toward animals. In fact, she's the one trained me to be a falconer. First she let me fly her kestrel. Then she gave me Roxanne and helped me train her." He grinned. "She wouldn't give up on me. She's sort of my parole officer, shrink, and friend. Joining ACE was Cheryl's idea. She said it was time for me to get back to academic life."

He stopped, as if he were coming to a particularly difficult revelation.

"I lied to you—to impress you, and because I wanted to share Roxanne with you. I'm not even allowed to have a falconry license yet. I'm not supposed to fly Roxanne until—this fall. That's what Cheryl was so pissed about—I wanted to take Roxanne out so I could show off for you. And then you hated it, after all my trouble!"

Marina looked down at the strong, tanned hand still gripping hers.

"That's quite a story," she said huskily. It was. It had cleared the air. Nick Menaker had a past, but now at least she knew what it was.

"So what do we do now? Can you take the artificial part off the foot? I mean, I think you should try to get up there. It's worth it."

Far from being offended at this bizarre suggestion, Nick seemed tickled by it.

86

"Take it off, she says. Like it was a sock. If I took it off I'd fall flat on my face. Man is a bipedal animal, kid." He slapped the offending foot. "Let's go. You take the water jug. I'll worry about making this hunk of junk behave."

"At least you can't break your ankle," said Marina.

"Sick joke." Nick poked her with his walking stick. But it was an affectionate poke.

At last they were climbing the ancient lichen-coated rocks, Marina leading, Nick behind her. They needed all their concentration just to maneuver.

As they rested between levels, Nick asked, "How'd the rocks get this way? Do you know?"

"I think some mountain belched them up in the form of lava."

A little while later . . . "Maybe they were underwater."

"Maybe. How's the foot doing?"

"So far, so good."

The discomfort with each other had disappeared. But even if it hadn't, they were focusing on the climb. Nick had to negotiate carefully. Marina knew he was putting out much more energy than she was. Each time he moved upward, he had to stop and rest the foot.

I didn't realize it would be so hard for him, Marina thought. *I certainly wouldn't bother, with a leg like that. I'd forget it. Watch a* National Geographic *special on pere-grines.*

Just then Nick slipped. Marina's grab for him was pure reflex. A swift reach for his arm and suddenly she was supporting his weight and hanging on for dear life with all her strength.

Oh please. Don't fall. Not here. We're all alone.

And then it was over. Nick had regained his balance. They were safe on the next ledge and Nick was thanking her and making jokes about how he owed his life to her and that they were bound together for all eternity.

They made their way up, up, and around, searching out the narrow crevices that afforded footing, standing erect to rest when they could gain a narrow plateau.

As they got closer to the place Marina remembered, she put her finger to her lips. So far they'd heard nothing, which must mean they had not alerted the falcons. Good. And then they heard the unmistakable cry of an eyass—a baby hawk.

Marina pointed silently to a tiny space between the rocks. It was so small that it was possible for only one person at a time to view the birds. She moved back so Nick could look through.

He put his glasses to the crack. Both falcons were there, standing side by side on the tiny piece of real estate they had reserved for their family. The female was feeding a chick what looked like the remains of a grouse. The male was watching the female dismember the food and feed it to the screeching offspring.

Marina watched his face take on a look of incredulity, then intense pleasure. His lips mouthed the words silently. *Fantastic. A white peregrine!*

She could imagine what he was thinking. That the brood had to be one of a kind. And then she saw a look of puzzlement on his face.

He turned to her and whispered, "I thought you said there were four eggs."

"There were."

"Take a look."

He sat back and Marina bent forward swiftly. There was only one chick in the nest!

What had happened? Had they been trapped in the shell, like the Harris hawks? They would have been too young to have taken flight. This one barely had flight feathers poking through the down of its wing tips and tail. There was the strange unseasonal storm. The eggs could have blown off the ledge and been dashed on the rocks below. And then she remembered the stranger. No. Wait a minute. No stranger anymore. Sam Spenser. And Cheryl. She had told Cheryl Harper where the birds were. Showed her on a map.

A queasy feeling hit Marina's gut. *The heat. Should have brought salt tablets.* She looked at Nick's flushed face. She knew he was dying to get his eye to that crack again. Reluctantly, she relinquished the viewing seat to him.

"I just don't know what happened," she whispered worriedly.

Nick seemed to have forgotten about numbers. He was riveted. She realized he had a much deeper attachment to hawks than she had. He was actually putting himself in the place of that falcon.

They sat there in near silence for perhaps a half hour, taking turns watching the falcons. Marina got thirsty and took a drink. She signaled to Nick to ask him if he wanted one but he just shook his head.

A few minutes later he whispered, "Can you believe how much bigger that female is?"

89

She didn't answer.

Nick's single-minded concentration on the falcons seemed out of proportion. If she were writing a story, she'd call it obsessive.

Nick sensed her watching him.

He frowned.

"What?"

She blushed.

"Nothing."

But her face gave her away.

"Ho-ho. You still don't trust me with your secret. You think I might . . ."

"No," she protested. "Nick—"

She started to tell him about Cheryl and the map, but he was already saying, "Come on. I've had enough."

He grabbed his walking stick and they started down the rocks. The going seemed even harder for Nick. About half-way down he said, without a trace of self-consciousness, "Hey, lady. Give us a hand, will you?"

Marina reached out. They threaded their way down, holding each other.

When they got to the cave ledge, they stopped to rest. This time, when Marina offered water, Nick accepted.

After he'd drunk, he said, "I was a little nervous up there. I thought the peregrines might come after us. I've had some experience with hawks defending their nests. And I've got the scars to prove it."

"The scar on your neck?"

"The very one."

"How did you get it?"

"It was in my younger, wilder days."

They sat companionably on a flat rock and ate peaches. But Marina couldn't stop thinking about the missing falcons. "If it isn't falconers taking the birds, who is it then?"

"Beats me." As if it were no concern of his.

"So where did Cheryl get Roxanne?"

The question triggered an outburst.

"Can't leave it alone, can you? You think birders and members of the Audubon Society are the only caring people in the whole world, right? And because I ride a motorcycle and Cheryl's a falconer that puts us among the bad guys."

"Nick, it's not that. But what happened to the other peregrine eggs up there?"

"Hey. Search my pockets."

"Come on, Nick. I'm serious."

"So am I. You don't trust me. I told you, that part of my life is *over*—o-v-e-r."

Marina pressed on.

"There's something I didn't tell you. The first time I was here, I saw a man looking at the nest through a high-powered scope. Guess what? The guy is living at Cheryl's. She says he's an old friend, but—"

Nick's cheek muscle twitched. It was clear he hadn't known about Sam Spenser! Still, he tried to pretend it didn't matter.

"If you're accusing Cheryl, forget it. And as far as this other guy is concerned . . . Look how hard it was for us to get up there. You think anyone would do that just to get a bird?"

"Maybe not you. But some people might. You remember what Cheryl said, that in some countries they'll pay a small fortune for a falcon?"

"They fell off the ledge. Period."

Relations were cool as they traveled down the rest of the way. They held each other, but it was for mutual safety. As they descended, Marina pointed silently to the easiest route. When they reached bottom, they still hadn't exchanged another word.

And then they saw the body.

CHAPTER

11

THE SMELL FIRST TOLD THEM IT WAS THERE. And then the caracaras. They swooped low, their red raptor heads thrust forward to have a look. Long afterward, Marina remembered that her last thought before they saw the body was that vultures have no feathers on their heads so they can keep clean as they eat.

There was no way this man could have been mistaken for a slumberer. Even beyond the gray color of his skin was the way the sun had already done its work on him— claimed bits of his chemistry that would eventually be recycled and returned somewhere in another form. *Matter is indestructible.*

He was tall and slim. His skin was dark, his hair straight and black. He still wore pants, a pair of nondescript greenish chinos. His shirt, if he had ever had one, was gone,

perhaps abandoned some time after he became disori-
ented. There were no signs of a canteen, of a hat, of any
equipment—watch, compass, anything that could have
been the instrument of his survival. He'd made the typical, fatal move of someone lost in the desert. Instead of
wearing more clothes and going into shade to rest and con-
serve body energy, he had stripped and exposed himself to
the full force of the merciless sun. Even his shoes were
gone.

All this Marina perceived, thought about. Nick may
have been thinking the same thing. But they did not
exchange a sound beyond Marina's initial high-pitched
keening and Nick's nauseated intake of air when they first
saw him slumped against the rocks.

Nick pulled the edge of the keffia around his face to
block out the odor. He dropped to his knees and felt the
man's pulse. But it had no connection with what they both
knew to be true. It was simply a concrete action to avoid
standing dumb in the sun looking at a corpse. And at last
Nick said, "He's dead. Probably been here a day or two.
Dehydration, I'd guess. Either that or he fell off that rock
face and hit his head. But there are no marks on him, at
least on this side."

He looked up at Marina.

"I don't think we ought to try to move him." It was a
question.

Marina shook her head.

Nick reached up and took off his backpack. "Let's cover
the—um—it—with our ponchos and go get the police."

"Okay."

94

But neither of them made a move.

"I — I'm not sure I can."

"I'll do it," said Nick.

"No, I'll help."

But as they started the grisly task, Marina began to cry. Nick's voice was gentle.

"Hey, kid, take it easy." He touched Marina's arm awkwardly, pushing her back a little, telling her in body language that she was released from active duty.

He knelt beside the dead man and began to wrap, as if he were readying a piece of meat for the freezer.

"This is the worst thing I've ever had to do in my life."

Marina, sitting back on her heels in the sand, nodded.

"Hey, wait a sec," she said. "There's dried blood on the back of his head."

"He must have got that when he fell."

She croaked out a thin wheeze of disagreement.

"If you're stumbling around on the ground, you usually fall forward. This bruise is on the back of his head."

"He could have fallen backward from up there." Nick nodded toward the rock face.

"What was he doing up there?"

"Look, Sherlock. Don't try to figure it out. Let's go get the professionals."

"Why don't you stay here," Marina offered. "I'll go."

Nick looked up, and it hit her. *Nick knows something terrible happened here. He doesn't want to stay alone.*

As if by agreement, they stood up together and started in the direction of the highway. Marina curbed her impulse to run ahead. She knew they should stay together

95

and that Nick's foot was bothering him. So she forced herself to go at his pace.

Nick began to offer his version of what had happened.

"He wouldn't have thought he was risking his neck. The desert—it's so tricky. Once I went for a ride out near Organ Pipe Monument with this kid. It was July and hot as a furnace. The car broke down and we were stuck up in the hills in the middle of nowhere with the temp a hundred fifteen or so and no shade."

"So what did you do?"

"We crawled under the car and stayed there all day until it was cool. Then we walked out to the highway. It was about six miles, I think. It would have been suicide to start out during the day. But even when you know the thing to do is to wait, it's hard to have the patience to do it. I remember us lying there playing Ghost and looking up at the muffler."

"So you think that guy back there died of wrong moves?"

"That's my guess."

"So what happened to his hat?"

"Probably wasn't wearing one."

"And he wasn't wearing shoes either?"

"He probably took them off. They could be half a mile away. The guy was wandering. They do that."

Marina was quiet. Then she said, "Maybe he was after the falcons."

Nick stopped. He hesitated, then said, almost to himself, "Maybe he was. I guess I haven't wanted to believe— I guess I thought it was amateurs—people like me, like I used to be, doing it for kicks. But now—"

Marina pressed him. "He fell almost directly under the nest. Don't you think that's a mighty strange coincidence?"

"I don't know. It sounds like a plot for ACE. But it's *real*. And it's hard to believe it's about falcons."

"Even if they're as rare as those birds are—were? Think what they'd be worth, falcons like that!"

"Right."

Marina felt her head pounding. She began to shout.

"You're a *rico*! You don't know about what people will do for money. A few years ago a kid was killed out in the desert. You know what he was doing? Collecting shell casings from a missile range. They're worth something because of the brass in them. He died for a few bucks' worth of brass."

Nick looked at her with something pleading in his face.

Why are you attacking me? he seemed to say.

Marina's face flamed.

"I'm sorry, Nick."

As if by mutual agreement they stopped talking. They walked in silence toward the pinstripes of telephone lines in the distance—the place where they would be able to unburden themselves of the awful knowledge of what lay at the base of Montenegro.

97

CHAPTER

12

AFTER THE HOT WHITE LIGHT OF THE
desert, Casa Cassidy seemed a cool and sheltering cave.
Nick went to the phone to call the police while Marina
went to find Isabel. She suddenly had a crying need to put
her head on the front of that familiar poppy apron and
inhale the faint perfume of sachet that was the smell of her
mother. She wanted to be patted and stroked, to hear Isabel's murmured incredulous *Verdad!* when she told her
about the dead man out in the desert.

But Isabel was nowhere to be found. Her kitchen workroom was spotlessly clean but empty. Marina searched the
house, looked for a note under the tomato magnet on the
refrigerator. Nothing. And the van was in the garage.

These murderers who had killed the man in the desert:
Suppose they had come to Casa Cassidy?

At that moment Marina began to sweat. Sweat poured out of her in tiny rivers and ran down her face, her legs, her arms. She knew it was the aftereffect of being in the dry, hot desert air and then coming into a cool room. The shock of the sudden cooling of her wet skin sent her into a paroxysm of shivering.

Just then Nick came into the kitchen. He, too, had the sweats. But he wasn't shaking the way Marina was.

"They'll be right over," he said. "Did you tell Isabel what happened?" And then, "What's the matter with you? You look as if you just stepped out of a freezer."

"My—Isabel isn't here. And she didn't leave a note. And the car is in the garage."

Nick frowned.

"She must be around somewhere. Probably took a walk." But his worried look worked against his words.

In the next few seconds Marina lived being a total orphan. What would she do without her mother?

Then she heard the sound of the police siren. And—oh, sunshine—coming across the sandy ground was Isabel, flushed from a neighbor's house, running up the driveway. When she saw the police car stopping in front of her house, she put her hand to her heart and gasped.

"What has happened?" And then when she saw Marina and Nick, "Oh! Thank God! I thought an accident!"

Isabel and the police learned what had happened at the same time. To Marina, the process seemed to proceed in slow motion. The detective in charge had a maddeningly deliberate way of talking. He punctuated each sentence with a sigh, as though the effort of carrying around his huge bulk and dealing with crime was too much for him.

He walked into the cool tile living room and settled himself in a small rush and leather Mexican chair. The leather groaned, protesting his bulk. The sound was loud in the quiet room. Marina was soaking wet and felt completely drained of energy.

"I'm Detective Murdoch," he said, as if his name were an additional burden.

I hope he doesn't ask me too much, Marina thought. *I don't even remember anything now.*

The detective began to ask questions. But before he asked for details about the location of the body, he seemed to want to know all about Marina and Nick. First Marina was subjected to a grilling, then Nick. Marina wondered if it were her imagination that he reacted strangely when Nick told him who he was. What could the Menaker name mean to this policeman?

At last he got around to asking about the dead man.

"You say he looked as though he had been there for some time?"

Nick looked tired, and his voice had that surly tone Marina had come to know. "Yes. But don't you want to go see for yourself? Shouldn't we get back out there?"

Murdoch refused to be rushed. He was taking notes in a tiny notebook in minuscule handwriting.

"Now let me get this straight. You were—bird-watching?" he asked, as if it were an activity that was both peculiar and suspect.

Nick had no patience for his plodding style.

"That's right. And if we go back there right away, you

may have a shot at finding someone *else* watching those birds."

The pen paused.

"You saw someone."

"We think someone—maybe the man himself—was after those birds," Marina said.

The detective looked at Marina coldly.

"Why? Did you know this man?"

"No. I—he looks—looked—like a foreigner, maybe an Arab. Er—from the Middle East."

"I know where Arabs come from," the detective said drily. "Anything else?"

"He looked like someone who didn't know much about the desert. He'd taken his clothes off."

The detective turned to a new page in his notebook, sighed slightly.

"An Arab who knew nothing about the desert," he said softly.

Marina blushed. He was making fun of her.

"Did you see any clothes around?"

"No."

"Did you search the area?"

"No."

Murdoch looked up.

"He could have taken them off somewhere else. Or," he whispered, "someone could have stripped him afterward, if his clothes had identification."

"I never thought of that."

Murdoch made her feel like an idiot.

The detective put his notebook in his pocket.

"That's the whole thing," he sighed. "Thinking."

He heaved himself out of the chair. "All right. Let's go have a look. We'll take the four-wheel-drive vehicle. That way we can drive right out to the site. I brought the coroner, so we can get some idea about time of death."

Now Isabel spoke for the first time.

"I will stay here," she said quietly. "Perhaps you would like a cold drink of tea before you go?"

"No, thank you, ma'am."

They prepared to go back out into the heat. But not before Isabel had a chance to whisper to Marina and Nick, "Take it easy, *muchachos. No tengas miedo.* Don't be afraid."

Marina directed them to Montenegro via the highway. There was a jeep trail that approached the hills from the other direction. She showed them how to get to it and at what point to leave it and cut across the desert floor. Finally they were there, and Nick was pointing out the body. It lay in its plastic shroud just as they had left it, a grayish lump, almost the color of the rocks surrounding it. Except for the flies circling and the caracaras, one would never have known.

Detective Murdoch's sighs took on new volume as the police medics unwrapped the body. He held a handkerchief to his nose. He puffed, wheezed, snorted. The notebook came out.

A police photographer took pictures. Murdoch left the immediate area to examine the surrounding rocks and to inspect the sand at the base of them. At intervals he would write something in the notebook, punctuating his penmanship with a sigh or two. Then he came back to the body. He knelt beside it. His knees cracked, and Marina was horrified to hear herself giggle.

No one looked at her.

Murdoch busied himself examining the dead man's belt buckle. He seemed to find the buckle fascinating. Still no one said anything. The coroner pulled on gloves and examined the body briefly. He placed the time of death as anywhere from eighteen to thirty-six hours before.

"Not very exact," Nick said in a stage whisper.

"Autopsy will pinpoint it," Murdoch said.

When he was finished with his minute examination of the corpse's clothing, he straightened up, sighing again. "Okay. Pack it in." He heaved a particularly heavy sigh.

If he sighs one more time, I may scream.

Carefully, Murdoch brushed the sand from his knees. He began to inspect the ground around the site. He appeared to be thinking of something. Suddenly he turned to Nick.

"You sure you don't know who this guy is?"

Nick was instantly tense, watchful.

"No. Should I?"

The detective shrugged and turned to Marina.

"What about you?"

"I never saw him before in my life."

Now there was an original line. Arnheim would have flunked her for using that one in a story.

Once again a sigh escaped the bellows of Detective Murdoch's lungs.

"Know what I think?" he asked softly. "I think we got

here Jimmy Toddy. U.S. citizen of Native American extraction. Game warden. Game and Fish reported him missing two days ago. That's an official-issue belt he's wearing."

Ai! Not an Arab smuggler. A Game Protector! One of the good guys!

Marina was badly shaken. Somehow she had been operating on the theory that the dead man was an outlaw, a foreigner who either had invaded a rival gang's territory or been killed by accident. Her imagination hadn't entertained the idea of a law enforcement officer. And she was thoroughly humiliated not to have recognized the dead man as a Native American.

The only thing she seemed to have been correct about was the theory of foul play.

"Doesn't this mean he was murdered?"

"He could have fallen. Tripped. If we find the rest of his clothes, it might give us a different picture." Detective Murdoch turned to the other officers. "Scout around, boys and girls. See what you can come up with. We're probably looking for a short-sleeved khaki shirt, a wide-brimmed hat, pair of desert boots and socks. They won't be easy to spot. But give it a shot."

"You don't know everything that has been happening here," Marina told Murdoch.

"I don't? So tell me."

She started with the news story about smuggling, but he waved his hand impatiently.

"I know all about that. What else have you got?"

Marina told him about the disappearance of the peregrine chicks. She told him about the mysterious phone call she had received. But when she went back to the beginning and started to tell about the man she had seen first at Montenegro, then at Cheryl's place, Nick interrupted her angrily.

"Leave Cheryl out of it. She's not involved."

"Better tell me everything," Murdoch said firmly. Marina noticed his sharp attention to Nick's behavior.

Marina was suddenly frightened. How had she gotten herself into this mess? Experience to put into a story was one thing. This was quite another. There was clear threat behind the detective's words. She went on talking, trying to remember anything that had happened that could be significant.

Detective Murdoch let her talk and made no comment. Just listened and made infinitesimal scratches in his little notebook. Finally, when she had run down her list of suspicious events, he said, "That's it?"

She nodded.

Suddenly, all that Marina wanted was to go home.

"May I call my mother on your car phone?"

"Sure. Go ahead." Murdoch nodded toward the radio car. Then he turned to Nick.

"What about you, son? Want to call your folks?"

"Not particularly."

Murdoch gave a long, pained sigh.

"You probably should. We got a printout on you. We understand you were in a little trouble a while ago that had to do with rare birds, right? Might be you'll need a lawyer."

The full force of what Murdoch was saying hit Marina like a sudden blow.

Of course! Nick's past was a matter of record! Just as she

had suspected him, *they* would suspect him. They were police, trained professionals. The idea that Nick could be involved had to be respected. And considered. But did it have to be believed?

Marina looked inward at her personal, updated, mental computer file on Nick Menaker. It was short and to the point.

He did something bad. He paid for it. Finis.

Some time in the last few hours of this day that seemed as if it had already been a year long, she had become convinced that Nick was a changed person. She knew with gut certainty that Nick could never have been part of this. Wild, maybe. And Nick had problems. But on balance he was— *I care a lot for him. I couldn't feel this way about him if he was rotten. And neither could Isabel.*

So. If Nick Menaker was someone she cared about, it was time to stand up and be counted. "Nick and I—Nick has been with me. We're always together. We were together all day today."

"So I gather." Murdoch's voice was soft. "But you don't sleep together."

Marina's face flamed with embarrassment.

Murdoch didn't seem to notice.

"Look," he said. "You're both into birds. And Menaker has been associated with birds in an illegal way. So think of it from my point of view. This here is a big wide network of little guys who work for big guys. The little ones that trade and sell information don't necessarily know what the big guns are doing. The little guys, they might just be in it for thrills or money or a rare bird of their own. We have to look at everything. At everybody. Every part of the situation. Think about it."

Marina went clammy with fear. This sighing detective from the police department suspected her, too. He suspected both of them were involved in some way with the bird smuggling and even with the dead man.

Marina looked over at Nick. How was he taking it? Hard to tell. One thing was sure. He wasn't saying much.

Anything you say may be held against you.

"Awright. Let's pull out of here. We'll drop you two back to the house." Murdoch turned to the other police officers. "Take the body to the morgue," he ordered. "I'll be there in a little while."

He shepherded Marina and Nick toward his car, sighing all the way.

CHAPTER

13

THE LAST THING MURDOCH SAID AS HE
dropped off Nick and Marina at the Cassidy house was that
they should "stick around for a while."

Nick was indignant. "Does that mean we're under suspicion?"

"No more than anyone else."

They walked into the house, weary. Isabel was waiting
for them with hot herb tea and gentle questions.

"So what is happening? Do they have any idea who did
this thing?"

"I don't know, *Madre*," Marina confessed. "I don't even
know whether we can trust the police."

And Nick added, "I don't know whether I'm supposed to
have done something or not. I don't even know what
Marina thinks. And I'm dead on my feet, besides. Dead on

my foot, I should say." He sank into the nearest chair.

Marina went over to him and stroked his hair lightly. She didn't even mind that Isabel was there. "I think—it'll be okay," she murmured. Nick put his head on her arm and looked across the room at Isabel.

His eyes were pleading.

"Mrs. C, do you know everything about me? Do you know what kind of boy your daughter is hanging around with? It's time we got everything out on the table here. I wouldn't want you to be shocked."

Isabel looked back at him calmly. Later, Marina thought how proud she was of her mother at that moment.

"I know you as a nice young man. All Marina has told me is you're sometimes crabby. If this is true, you might think about improving your disposition. For the rest, if you did something, it is in the past and it's over. I trust you. And now I'm going to bed." So saying, Isabel left the room.

She had just stepped out of the room when the phone rang. It was Cheryl. Through the haze of her fatigue, Marina heard the husky voice saying, "Hullo. Marina? Is that you?"

"Cheryl, we were about to call you. Something's happened."

Nick signaled he was going to pick up the phone in the other room.

Let me tell her, he pantomimed.

Nick got on the phone.

"Hey, Cheryl, I'm here, too. Listen, you know a guy named Jimmy Toddy, Game and Fish?"

There was a pause. Then Cheryl said, "Yeah. I know him. He's been over here from time to time, bugging me about bird smugglers. Persistent little cuss. What about him?"

Nick broke the news of Jimmy Toddy's death. Cheryl Harper's response was anything but quiet.

A stream of words poured from the telephone receiver, followed by a long silence, as if Cheryl had her hand over the receiver and was talking to someone.

Then at last, in a totally different, tougher voice, she said, "Toddy was an accident waiting to happen. The way he walked around in the desert. And he traveled alone, too. That was a mistake. Game Protectors oughta travel in pairs. In case anything happens. The little jerk." There was a fresh barrage. And then the sound of crying. And then silence. Cheryl had either run out of steam or—

"Let me talk now," Marina begged Nick.

Nick hung up his phone.

Marina tried to focus on what she wanted to find out. "Cheryl, do you think Jimmy Toddy had discovered something? About the smuggling, I mean."

"How should I know? Game and Fish doesn't confide in me."

She's not telling everything she knows. Marina made a few more efforts to get some facts about Toddy from Cheryl. But Cheryl's answers were guarded.

Finally Marina asked, "So what did you call about in the first place?"

"What?" Cheryl seemed distracted. Then, "Oh. Yeah. I

wanted to tell you that Harry and Harriet Hawk's offspring are doing fine. Their feathers are growing in nicely. They'll be branchers one of these days—climbing out of the nest to sit on a perch. I actually called to say that there are no problems here. No problems. Some joke. Ha." Her voice broke. "Listen. I can't talk now. Someone just came in."

Someone, yeah. And I know who the someone is. Sam Spenser.

"Listen. Cheryl, you still there?"

"Eyah. I'm here."

She could hear the impatient drumming of Cheryl's nails.

She wants to get off the phone.

"Cheryl, did you show anyone that map I drew of where the peregrines were nesting?"

No answer.

"Cheryl, did you know that I saw Sam Spenser at Montenegro before I saw him at your house? Cheryl, he knows about that platinum peregrine. Who else knows, Cheryl? Besides you and Sam?"

Still no answer. But there was conversation in the background.

And finally Cheryl was saying in a thin, tight voice, "Listen. You two get some sleep. Then you had better come over here tomorrow, ten o'clock. We'll talk."

She hung up before Marina could answer.

Marina could barely keep her eyes open long enough to tell Nick what Cheryl had said.

"Why don't you stay over?" she offered. "You look so tired."

Nick shook his head.

"Thanks. But I think I need to go home. I have to tell my father about all this. Before someone else tells him. "Good night, Marina." Suddenly Nick leaned over and kissed her. His lips brushed her mouth, and then he was gone.

She went in and flopped down on her bed.

Just my luck. The first time a guy kisses me I'm so wiped out I hardly know what's happening!

The next thing she knew the morning sun was streaming into her window, and Nick was banging on her bedroom door, exhorting her to rise and shine.

When they got to the raptor center, the first surprise was seeing Murdoch's car in the driveway. The second was seeing him with Sam Spenser, and the two of them acting like old buddies. But by far the biggest shock was the two men in Western shirts and boots who introduced themselves as agents of the United States Fish and Wildlife Service.

It was altogether a strange gathering. And the hostess did not seem to be enjoying her party.

"So what gives, Cheryl? Is this the day we all get the straight story?"

Nick was tense, and his voice was loud in the room. He sensed that for some reason he was the focus of attention.

Cheryl avoided his eyes. "Eyah. Now, Nick, don't get mad, okay? We thought it was time you two knew what was going on."

She glanced at Sam Spenser as if asking for help. None was forthcoming. She took a deep breath.

"When this—um—wildlife smuggling began to get out of hand, they started an investigation and—um—the government asked me to cooperate. I—" She looked away. "At first I didn't want to get involved. I said no. But then when Jimmy Toddy got into it, and he said he needed help, well—" Her voice broke. "He was a buddy and—I didn't see how I could *not* do it when he was risking his neck. Sam Spenser here was sent to be my—to work here and—try to make contact with the—anyone who wanted to buy and sell illegal birds. Sam used to be—um—he used to deal in illegal wildlife before he became—before he started to work for the government. We kind of—put out the word in the falconry community that—we'd sell wild endangered species and other things—for a price."

"Oh, no. Be part of a sting! How could you? Especially after you gave us that big song and dance about the government and the little guys and how everyone was going to be put on the spot and how the Feds were harassing you. Great, Cheryl! Nice con job!" Nick looked positively sick.

Cheryl made believe she hadn't heard his tirade.

"We called around here and there and—um—put ads in the paper. We also—uh—called certain people and fished around to see who was interested, to try to sniff out the middlemen. We hoped they'd lead us to the top dogs."

Nick's voice was ominously flat. "So that's why I got that call last week, isn't it?" He turned to Cheryl and said softly, "I don't believe you. You even tried to trap me."

So Nick got a call, too. He didn't tell me. And I didn't tell him.

Sam cut in. "Wait a sec. It wasn't Cheryl's idea. It was

mine. We had to be sure you were clean. We just ask, remember. We don't force you to do something illegal."

Now it was Marina's turn to be angry. "So I suppose you made up that dopey contest, didn't you?"

"What contest?"

"The one I got a call about. Last week."

"That one didn't come from us. We don't know who that was. We'd like to, though. We need everything that anyone knows. That's one of the reasons we wanted you to come here today."

"Let me finish, will you?" Cheryl was rapping out a tattoo on the table with her nails.

"We weren't getting anywhere until—you're going to hate this, Marina—until you told us about the platinum peregrine. Sam knew there was a pair of falcons up there somewhere, but he never saw them close up. And he didn't know about the nest. After you told us, we realized they could be the perfect bait. A peregrine and the chance for an albino.

"Sam and Jimmy cooked up the idea. They figured they'd work it two ways—Jimmy would plant information about the place and then stake it out—see who would turn up for a little do-it-yourself wildlife theft. He'd wait until they went for the chicks and then nab them."

"You had no right!"

Cheryl continued, "We also spread the story—untrue, of course—that the Three R had illegally taken two of the eggs and was incubating them for sale on the black market. We figured the smugglers might decide it was easier to buy the eyasses from us illegally than to climb up there.

114

But we reasoned that either way, we had spread the net, and we'd catch someone."

"Do you have any idea what happened out there in the desert?"

"Not for sure. We found truck tracks. That much we know; someone was there. But we also know Jimmy had a good hiding place in a cave halfway up or so."

He could have been in the same cave I hid in the day of the rain.

"I don't think he really believed the thieves would try to get up the mountain, though. He figured that when they saw how hard it was to climb, they'd bite on the other bait. But they must have had equipment for climbing. They must have been thrilled when they saw four eyasses for the taking. We don't know why they left the one. Probably to keep the pair there. They knew the parents wouldn't hang around if all the chicks were gone. The smugglers might even have been figuring on coming back for the female. She's enormously valuable for breeding."

"More likely, they could only get three of the young before they were attacked by the birds. Or by Jimmy."

"I think Jimmy may have given himself away somehow. He couldn't have known they were there. He had a radio, and he would have been in touch with us."

"So maybe he caught them, and then they overpowered him."

Murdoch joined the conversation. "The coroner said Jimmy was struck on the side of the head with a hard object. Could have been a rock. But the blow didn't kill him. The desert did. They just must have undressed him

115

and left him unconscious, to die of exposure. Given the heat during the day, it didn't take long."

Now it was Marina who wanted to believe that it had not been a murder. "Isn't it possible he fell and hit his head?"

"It's possible. But if he had fallen down the mountain, there'd be other marks on his body. Scrapes. Lacerations. Even a broken bone. We didn't see anything like that. We think he saw them go up to take the peregrine eyasses. He wanted to nab them with the goods. So he came down and waited near the bottom for them."

"And then they killed him?" Nick asked.

"I don't think they planned it that way. They just wanted to get away and—in the struggle—"

Sam Spenser said, "They hit him. Or he tripped. If I know Jimmy, he probably was trying to make a capture without hurting the eyasses. So he went in with a drawn gun and hoped they'd give up."

"Where are the chicks?" Marina asked.

Hesitation all around.

"We don't know."

"You don't know!" Marina exclaimed. "Well, if you don't know, I'll tell you. They're across the border or on a plane. Or they're already dead. You sacrificed a man's life and the lives of six endangered birds for your stupid little sting. Some logic. You take what could be the rarest birds ever and . . . You call yourselves wildlife law enforcers. You just like to play cops and robbers. You like wiretaps and double agents and entrapment. You get off on that stuff."

One of the Western shirts broke in on her tirade. "Be realistic, Ms. Cassidy. We're talking here about traffic in hundreds of falcons. Isn't it worthwhile to sacrifice a few to save a great many? Anyway," he added coolly, "we never thought it would turn out this way."

"If you didn't, you're not too smart," Nick said. "It's really great. Save endangered species by trashing them. And you're supposed to be the good guys."

Everyone studied the floor. Finally Murdoch broke the silence with one of his sighs.

"Son, you may be right. There have been mistakes made. There may have been leaks. But right now we have a murder on our hands. Whoever did it isn't going to go back to the mountain after this. And somehow they've found out that Sam and Cheryl are working for us. All our moles have gone into their holes. We need a new angle. Fresh personnel."

Suddenly everyone was looking at Nick Menaker.

CHAPTER

14

"OH, NO. NO, YOU DON'T. I WON'T TOUCH THIS. Not with a ten-foot pole."

Seeing Marina's puzzled look, Nick said, "Don't you get it? They want *me* to be part of their sting. They goofed it up, so now they want to use me."

Cheryl winced, as though Nick's words were aimed directly at her.

"Please, Nick. Don't look at it that way. Think about it. A guy has been murdered. Maybe we can find out who did it. Maybe we can even get the falcons back."

But Nick was adamant. He shouted at her, "You were the one who told me not to get mixed up in anything. To keep my nose clean. No way," he kept saying. Then he turned to the law enforcement officers. "There's no way I'm going to work for you guys. I remember you from when I was on the wrong side of the law. I hated you then, and I don't love you now. You find a guy like Sam Spenser, who used to sell illegal birds, and you use him. He finds you a few falconers who break the law, and you think you've done your job. You never get to the big guys. Meanwhile, thousands of endangered animals of all kinds are getting in and out of here. And where are you guys? Playing games."

Murdoch was sighing again. A bad sign. Marina had noticed that Murdoch's sighs were inevitably followed by something you didn't want to hear.

"Fish and Wildlife feels you owe them, son," he told Nick.

He means the Feds. The silent ones standing there in their Western boots.

"They bent over backward when you were in your trouble. You could have gotten a jail term for what you did. Instead they let you off with a fine and the chance to work your way back into the falconry community. They even overlooked the fact that you recently flew a falcon without a license."

Nick looked at Cheryl accusingly.

"It wasn't me," she protested miserably. "I came down hard on you because I was afraid we'd both get into trouble. A Game and Fish guy saw you and reported it. It was just after the news of the smuggling ring, so they were looking at falconers more than usual."

Murdoch continued unperturbed. "Now, son, you're supposed to get your bird and your license back in the fall. That can't happen if you don't cooperate. I mean, if you don't help us, we can't help you, now, can we?"

Marina looked at Nick, sitting with his head in his hands. What was he thinking about? Choices. Roxanne. Of course. His beautiful bird. If he didn't do what they said, he'd lose her forever. Even before he answered, Marina knew what his decision had to be.

"You guys are something else," Nick said. "You don't leave a person anywhere to go."

He turned toward Cheryl, hostility and contempt in his face.

"And you. Giving me all that crud about caring about others and love and doing good for the animals. You're full of it, Cheryl, you know that?"

Marina heard herself defending Cheryl.

"It's not her fault, Nick. Don't you see they've got her, too?"

"That's it, Nicky," Cheryl said bitterly. "They'll take away my breeding license."

Sam Spenser was a practical man. He knew what buttons to push. Now he said, "Go tell Sarah Toddy about choices. Mention to her about ways and means." And when they sat in shocked silence, "Okay, come on. Let's lighten up. This will all be over in a couple of weeks, and we can all relax."

Silence.

"So what do you say, kid? Are you in?" Spenser asked.

You could barely hear Nick's answer.

"Yeah. I'm in."

Now he turned to Marina.

"What about you, Marina? We think they're aware of

120

you, and you could help give additional weight to Nick's cover. Will you do what's necessary?"

If Nick is in, then . . .

"Okay."

Cheryl looked relieved.

"So," Nick asked, "what is it exactly that we're supposed to do?"

Sam Spenser laid out the plan.

"We've got two jobs. One is to get those people before they leave the country. The other is to get the peregrine eyasses back, if we can. What we think will bring them in is an offer they can't refuse. Someone says 'I'm willing to pay more for the birds than you can get anywhere else.'"

"How are we supposed to know they have the birds?"

"We'll keep it simple. Tell as much of the truth as we can. Marina told you that there were rare peregrines up on the mountain. The two of you went up there to get them. There was only one left, so you didn't take it, because you wanted to keep the peregrines in the area. When you came down you found the body. You reported it. Then you decided to try to find out who got the birds because you wanted them for yourselves. You're rich, Nick, so it's plausible."

"You mean *I'm* buying the birds?"

"That's it. But don't forget, Marina's in, too."

"Why?"

"More believable. They know she was up there. They know you see her. She would have to be in."

"Okay. How do we get this story around?"

"You go to the places where you hung out before. Go

121

where the motorcycle crowd goes. Where the hunters go. Where the playboys hang out. *You* know."

"That's a lot of different places."

"It's a lot of acting, too. Remember, you have to be convincing. You're a rich sleaze, you've got a bankroll, and you want to buy your girlfriend a bird."

"Yeah. Okay. So I get the word out. Then what?"

"Then you wait to hear. And you stay away from us and from the Three R. We don't want them to make any connections."

"How about an ad?"

"Good. But we'll need to move fast. I'd like to try to catch this group before they move on out."

Soon after that, the meeting was over.

Nick and Marina left together. And as soon as they did, Nick turned to her.

"Hey, Marina, how come you're getting caught up in this? They can't force you. They don't have much on you. You could stand clear. You sure you want to do it?"

Marina nodded. "I'm sure I can't quit now. I've got to stay with it. I want to see how the plot winds up. Besides, I really care about getting back those birds."

Marina studied Nick's face. Obviously, neither of her reasons was the one Nick was looking for.

She hadn't told him the whole truth, and nothing but the truth.

"And the other thing is, I care about you, Nick Menaker."

She said it so softly he had to bend down to hear it.

CHAPTER

15

FOR NICK, THE NEXT FEW WEEKS BECAME A time to re-create Nick Menaker. He approached the task methodically, as if reconstituting his old image were an assignment. He hung out in his former haunts and took up with his old hunting buddies. He let it be known that the kid had reverted to his former wild ways. That he was interested in deals. Any kind.

Marina helped him concoct some of the details of his new persona. "How about: Your father has kicked you out of the house because he doesn't approve of me."

"Why?"

"Oh—um—because I'm the caterer's daughter. Rich boy, poor girl?"

"I don't think so. That plot's old. But the 'kicking out' part is good. And believable. Trouble is, my dad will deny it if anyone asks him. And if I tell him not to, then I have to explain the whole sting to him. And that's not good."

"How about you need money for drugs?"

"I don't want to have to pretend I'm a druggie. It's too hard an act to pull off. And it's simple to check out a drug story. It's a fraternity and the members know one another."

They worked on the plot harder than they had ever worked in Arnheim's class. Finally they put together a story that seemed to ring true. Nick Menaker's father was tired of supporting him. He had a new girlfriend with expensive tastes. Both he and the girl were into falcons and didn't mind buying endangered species. They were prepared to deal.

That was the story Nick spread around. Then he placed a series of ads in hunting magazines and trade journals. By careful wording, he was able to convey an interest in buying and selling rare raptors without appearing to be outside the law. Nick knew the code of this subworld well.

He started out hating what he was doing. But after he had come to terms with his own role in the sting, he began to be invested in its success. Nick needed to win—not for his falconry license or relief from his parole situation—not even for Roxanne or for the rare peregrines he had glimpsed that once on the mountain. He was doing it for himself, and he was going to do it well.

Marina's impatient temperament found Nick's slow, thorough method frustrating. "Every day that goes by gives us less chance to find those peregrine eyasses."

"I can't change my personality overnight. These guys are playing for big stakes and they're not going to trust my bouncing back and forth from bad boy to good citizen and then back again unless I plant the idea gradually. It has to be logical, otherwise they'll be scared off. We may have to live with the idea that the peregrine eyasses are gone, and concentrate on trying to get Jimmy Toddy's murderers and maybe stop further traffic in rare falcons."

The days passed. The calendar inched into summer. Gradually the stir caused by the death of Jimmy Toddy began to dissipate, like the news of the latest crime wave in Phoenix or like the cool breeze that occasionally stirred the desert air. Officially, the death was listed as "under further investigation." But unofficially the police were saying that heat prostration had been the cause of death. All part of the sting, but Sarah Toddy and the Native American community had not been advised. They complained about the way the case was being handled.

Meanwhile, Serenity settled into its summer state of quiet torpor. The resorts closed; Arizonians who could afford it went up to Flagstaff or down to the Coronado mountains or out to the Caribbean.

In the cool, half-buried bedroom in the back of her house, Marina turned to her writing. She wrote about a man she called Jimmy Toddy. She made him up, created him out of her imagination as the hero of a fictional story. It was as if, by conjuring a character named Jimmy Toddy on Will's old portable Smith-Corona, she brought him back to life. *Write about what you know,* Arnheim had said. She realized for the first time what that really meant. It meant *use* what you know as the take-off point. Then spin it out from there. But how?

She wrote about the nest of falcons on the bleak mountain of random rock, and about the disappeared nestlings—the little *desaparecidos* she had never actually seen. One night she dreamed of a huge bird. It looked like a figure from one of the fairy tales she had read when she was a little girl. In the dream, as in the story, a princess wearing a robe of bird feathers was snatched by the King of the Underworld. The image was so vivid and so frightening that it woke her. She stared into the dark, her heart pounding. Finally she understood it. The white-robed princess was a white bird—the platinum peregrine, or her offspring. The Marsh King, the hideous figure that she remembered from her childhood—that was the force of darkness, whoever it was, that preyed on the royal birds. She would use that image in her story of the peregrines, just as she had used the images that had come out of the real experience.

As for Isabel, her catering business always dropped off in summer. But Isabel seemed to welcome having time on her hands. Instead of brooding, she cooked. And when all the *sopa pollo*, the Chocolate Sinbads, the fragrant breads that fit had been stored in the big steel freezer, she turned back to her clay pots. Any morning you could find her at the wheel, centered on clay, creating jars and jugs and plates of the most original and incredible beauty. And they were not for sale. Isabel was working only for herself out there in the little studio behind the house.

Nick had dropped out of writing class. "Doesn't fit my image," he said. When he was not making contacts at bars and meetings, or checking his post office box for replies, or answering ads that other falconers had placed, he could always be found around the Cassidy house. The word was out in the subcommunity of dealers in wildlife that you could reach Nick Menaker by letter at Box 1102, Serenity, or by phone at Casa Cassidy.

And so they waited, the three of them. But nothing happened. *Nada*, as Isabel would say. It was as if the falcon smuggling operation had gone into the rocks like chuckwallas retreating from the heat.

One day, restless and bored sitting by the mute telephone, Nick suggested he take lessons in pottery to pass the time. Without any embarrassment, Isabel took him on as a paying student. From then on the daily routine changed. When Nick was there in the morning he disappeared into Isabel's workroom until lunchtime, while Marina worked on her writing. Under Isabel's gentle guidance, Nick began to produce his own pots, full of vigor and originality. But from Isabel he seemed to learn more than the techniques of working clay. He began to relax. His occasional sullenness disappeared and his disposition improved as he unburdened himself into her sympathetic ear. Marina would hear them, talking softly or laughing together.

Watching Isabel with Nick one day, Marina suddenly had a revelation.

She brings out the best in everyone. That's what it is. That's her secret—why everyone loves her. She doesn't make judgments; she believes in your worth and you want to live up to her assessment of you.

Marina looked at these two people whom she cared

127

about, the blond head and the dark one bent over the wheel, and she felt a surge of happiness.

Nick looked up and caught her expression, and her mood.

"If we're lucky they'll never call," he said simply. "And we can just hang out, being creative and eating good."

But the idyllic situation couldn't last. By the end of the second week, the silence was beginning to be oppressive. And by the third week, nerves were starting to be raw. Lunch break turned into gripe time. Nick started it.

"I'm going to tell them I want out. We're not getting anywhere."

"You can't expect instant results." Marina tried to sound encouraging but wound up sounding preachy.

"Sometimes I think your only interest in this whole thing is so you can write a story about it and show off for old Arnheim."

Isabel stepped in to change the subject and act as peace-maker.

"You know—this morning as I worked with my clay, I was thinking about the substance itself. Clay has a kind of life of its own." Her voice became animated. Her audience sensed that she was about to tell a story. "Did you know that if you take a lump of clay and hit it with a hammer, it releases ultraviolet energy for a month? The scientists don't quite understand its chemical composition, but it is alive. And some people are saying now that life may have started in clay."

Nick was immediately distracted and intrigued by this idea. Isabel had accomplished her purpose.

"Hey! Life? Give me a break." He knew scoffing at Isabel would provoke further discussion.

"No. I mean it! If you think about what a life form is, it's energy from the environment that can make chemical changes happen. That describes clay. And of course that's the story that the ancient people tell—that the animals and the fish and the birds were all fashioned by God, or the gods, from clay. The Maya, the Old Testament prophets, the Native Americans—they all say clay. So the scientists and the spiritual leaders may agree for once!"

Marina turned to her mother.

"What about the Australian aborigine idea—the one that says that the creatures of the world were *sung* into existence?"

Now Nick entered the discussion.

"Maybe the ancients sang as they were shaping the clay and that breathed life into the forms. In fact, didn't you hear Isabel and me caroling over the clay this morning?"

Isabel laughed. "I was teaching Nick the real Spanish words to 'La Cucaracha,' which is actually about a cockroach that has lost her marijuana weed."

Marina shook her head, laughing.

"I don't know, Isabel. I think you're corrupting my friend here . . ."

And then the phone rang.

CHAPTER

16

"I'LL GET IT."

Nick picked up the phone in the next room. They heard him say, "Yes, it is." Then he closed the door.

Fifteen minutes later, Marina and Isabel were still sitting at the table over their iced tea. Nick opened the door. They looked up expectantly.

He said a single word.

"Bingo!"

Someone had called, in answer to one of the ads. The bait had been swallowed—or at least was being nibbled on, if the caller was to be believed.

"He said he's interested in 'sharing artifacts of rare falcon observation and study.' That's the phrase I used in my ad. He didn't say a single word about buying or selling a bird on the phone, but then again, he wouldn't. He's using this call to check out my background. 'What sort of observations have you made,' that sort of thing. I told him I had some pictures of a rare white hybrid. I said I sure would like to have that bird, or its offspring. But I mentioned it as a sort of an aside. He could read it as just a fantasy, if he's a legitimate falconer. Which I don't think he is. I may be wrong, but he seemed to know I had been in trouble with the law."

Marina felt a prick of fear. "How could you tell?"

"When I told him my name, he acted as if he recognized it."

"So how did you leave it?"

"He said he'd call me again. That means he needs to talk it over with someone else and check me out some more."

Isabel had listened quietly, as she always did. From the beginning, she had not intruded herself into the sting, although she had been told about it. But now she saw fit to speak.

"I'm worried about something. These people who called—could it be they think your business is blackmail? The way that ad was worded—what if they think you have photographs of them—evidence that they murdered Jimmy Toddy? Isn't that possible?"

It was certainly a sobering thought.

There were no more calls that day. Nick fumed, went over his conversation with the caller to try to figure out if he'd said something that had scared him off, or had given himself away.

And then the following morning the second call came. This time Nick left the door open so they could listen. Marina and Isabel heard him say, "Yes. This is Nick Menaker." And then, "I see. Yes. I'd be happy to share information about falcons with you. No. Tomorrow is no good for me. Let's make it next week. I'd like to take a look at your—artifacts—and chat with you. But I'm in no hurry. I'm a collector, you understand. I don't want anything that—"

The phone caller seemed to protest.

"Well, I suppose, if you're leaving town—maybe I could switch my schedule to accommodate you. Tonight? Mmm. All right. Where? That'll be okay, I guess. And in case I'm interested in any of your—maybe we can arrange a further meeting sometime. Right."

He hung up.

Marina was almost bursting. "Nick, are you nuts? Why were you so casual? You can't meet with them until 'next week'? Those birds could be dead or departed for parts unknown by next week."

"I know." Nick fingered his earring thoughtfully. "I had to take the chance. I don't want them to think I'm pressing too hard. They'll get suspicious. They could be dealers, just fishing. But the fact that they're in such a hurry—"

"Means that they want to get the birds off their hands and split. Which probably means they've got young birds, and they're having a hard time keeping them alive."

Nick looked from Isabel to Marina.

"By the way, I should tell you that the last call was from a woman. So at least one member of the gang is female."

"It's nice to know there's no discrimination in the illegal wildlife trade," said Marina.

"Also, both callers had foreign accents that I don't recognize. They're not Hispanic, I know that much."

132

"Good," said Isabel, as if that reflected well on all people of Spanish heritage.

"I have a date to meet them tonight."

"Where?"

"The Alhambra Hotel. Scottsdale."

"Wow. Must be a good business if they can afford to stay there."

"They probably aren't staying there. We're supposed to meet in one of the big rooms. This will be an exploratory for them. They won't bring the birds even if they have them. They'll bring photos or some other evidence. And they won't show them to me until they've thoroughly checked me out. Then we'll cut a deal and then we'll arrange the transfer of the birds. That's when Murdoch and the others will move in."

Marina was both impressed and repelled by the fact that Nick seemed to know so much about how to handle an illegal operation.

He caught her looking at him. As if he could read her thoughts, he said gently, "Hey, don't let it get to you, sweet face. Think about it this way. It's one of the fringe benefits of that experience stuff you're so crazy for. It's what makes me so perfect for the job."

And then he added, "By the way . . . I told them I was bringing my girlfriend. It's good. It fits with what they've heard."

Isabel started to protest. But Marina quickly said, "This is it, Mom. This is what we've been waiting for. Nick has to go and it has to be better for him not to go alone. Besides, they won't do certain things if both of us are there."

133

"Like what things?" Isabel was plainly concerned. "You are going to call Murdoch and the others, aren't you?"

Nick looked uncomfortable.

"I don't have to tell them, Isabel. They have a tap on your phone. I've already talked to them and they'll be around. But we're all agreed that they won't move in tonight. We don't want to scare off these people. They're our only leads so far."

"What if they're not the ones who have the peregrines?"

"That could be. Maybe they have some other birds they've stolen or bought illegally. In any case, they don't sound legit. We'll have to see."

The rest of the afternoon dragged. No one could work. Nick went home to shave and get dressed. Marina spent a considerable amount of time washing her hair. Even Isabel left her clay and bustled aimlessly in the kitchen, making a salad that neither she nor Marina was hungry for when finally it was dinnertime.

Marina was more than slightly sick to her stomach. She tried to talk herself out of it, to reason with the panic that threatened to come up into her throat.

This is what you wanted. Experience. Adventure. Here it is, right where you live. And you won't be alone. You'll be with Nick. And the Feds will be riding backup. But still the fear lay there like an ugly beast. To keep it at bay, she put her mind on trivia. "I don't know what to wear. What do you wear to meet a couple of murderers?"

"Alleged," Isabel murmured.

"What?"

"Alleged murderers. You don't know that these people are the ones. They may just be small-time criminals, not

134

murderers. You can't jump to conclusions."

"There you go again," said Marina irritably. "Giving everyone the benefit of the doubt. Maybe you'd like to take up a collection for the civil rights of these cruds."

"Maybe. I understand about crime in the streets. But not every criminal is a murderer."

"This time you're way off the mark, *Madre*. These are genuine bad guys, capable of murder. I can feel it."

Isabel came back at her quickly. "If that is so, then you and Nick are in grave danger. You had better call off this expedition right now and let the police handle it themselves."

Marina knew why her mother was being so argumentative. Isabel was worried about her. She was actually debating with herself over whether Marina and Nick were in danger. Somehow the fact that her mother was worried for her took some of Marina's own fear away. Isabel was in charge of the worry department. And Isabel wouldn't let anything happen to her. She, Marina, could go and do some exercise and take a shower.

The combination of vigorous exercise and a relaxing shower took away some of her tension. She dressed slowly. She had decided to wear a pair of red linen pants and a white and red cotton sweater and sandals. For a change, she did her eyes, and put high color on her cheeks and mouth.

I'm going to Scottsdale to play bad old Nick Menaker's moll. Gotta look the part.

When she came out of her room, Marina covered her nervousness by kidding around. "I'm incognito tonight as you can see. Eye makeup, lipstick, crimped hair—no one

135

will recognize me."

"You make a very nice moll," was Isabel's verdict.

And Nick said, "Do you always look so gorgeous when you go out catching criminals?"

Suddenly the whole thing seemed silly and melodramatic. What if these people were really going to show them pictures of hawks and nothing more? What if they were just falcon freaks? Wouldn't that be wild? Then again, maybe adventure always seemed ordinary when you were actually living through it. Maybe adventure was discomfort seen in retrospect.

A new disquiet sneaked into her consciousness. Supposing they discovered that she and Nick were phonies. What would happen to them? The same thing that had happened to Jimmy Toddy?

Nick read her face. "Don't worry. There's backup. I told you."

"But how will the backup know what's going on in the hotel room?"

"They have that room wired."

"Oh."

"Time to go," Nick said.

"Is there anything I should do?" asked Isabel. "Anyone I should call at a certain time?"

Nick glanced at his watch. "Yeah. If you don't see us or hear from anyone by ten o'clock, call this number."

They climbed into the Land Rover. When Marina looked back, Isabel was in the doorway, wearing her poppy apron. Just standing there, with that Mayan statue look on her face.

CHAPTER

17

MARINA HAD NEVER BEEN TO THE ALHAMBRA Hotel. It was enormous. Six-hundred-odd rooms in a Spanish-style castle sprawled across acres of scrubland that had been completely transformed into a desert Camelot. They drove up a tree-lined drive. On one side a sweep of green stretched to the horizon. If knights had come riding over the crest of the hill, it would not have surprised her. But on closer inspection she saw that the green was a golf course and the castle moat was really a decorative water-filtration system. The historic look that mimicked the great Spanish building was only a facade.

But beyond the movie set exterior one got a totally different feeling. Once Marina and Nick had turned the Land Rover over to the parking attendant and were inside, they might as well have been in a hotel in New York, Chicago, or Las Vegas. Pure impersonal glitz. The contrast was not lost on Marina.

Never can tell what's inside by the outside. As with old Nick Menaker.

They stopped for a minute at the entrance to the huge room to look around and get their bearings. The lobby was crowded. There was a steady murmur of talk, and a stream of traffic going in and out of the mighty carved entrance doors. But Nick and Marina felt strangely alone and vulnerable. For all they knew the people they had come to see were there, somewhere in the crowd, watching them.

"Is someone from our backup in here?"

"I don't think so. I think they're set up in a van in the parking lot."

"Are you sure they'll be able to hear?"

"Yes. They scoped out the place this morning. Come on." Nick took her arm. "We're supposed to meet them in the Granada Room."

They made their way to the ornate map on the wall, which told them where they were standing and showed them the route along the elegant carpeted hallways to the Granada Room. It was on another floor and down a long empty corridor that stretched into the distance like a surrealist painting.

Marina giggled nervously.

"What's so funny?"

"I don't know," Marina admitted. "It's just so weird meeting them in a place like this."

"Not really," Nick whispered. "If they're the foreign falconers themselves, and not middlemen, they're probably very well-to-do types. They could even be sheiks. Oil millionaires. They'd be used to being in places like this."

"Do you really think they'd meet with you themselves? The top guys?"

"No, I don't. I don't know what to think. You're right. It *is* weird to bring us here."

They were at the door of the Granada Room.

Nick took a deep breath. "Be that as it may. Here goes."

He opened the door quickly, and they stepped inside.

The room was empty.

They walked in, their footsteps quiet on the thick carpets. Obviously, this was a room to be hired for a party. But at the moment the pale red velvet chairs were neatly stacked at one side of the room, the polished tables were bare, and the small ballroom floor was deserted. The only hint of human life in the whole room were the portraits that lined the walls. They were all of Spanish noblemen, done in the style of El Greco. They stared down at Marina and Nick with royal contempt.

"Are you sure they said the Granada Room?"

"I'm positive. I wouldn't make a mistake on a thing like that."

Marina looked at her watch.

"Actually, we're a little early. Two minutes."

"Yeah." Nick ran his hands through his hair.

"Maybe we should sit down."

"Yeah, why not."

They lifted two of the velvet chairs off the stack and sat.

"I feel stupid," Marina said. "The two of us all alone in this big space."

Nick looked at his watch again.

"They should be here by now. Maybe something went wrong. Maybe Murdoch and the others traced the phone call and . . ."

"Ssh," Marina hissed.

"What's the matter with you? There's no one here."

"*They* could have the room bugged, too," she whispered.

"Sure. Behind the portraits, right?"

"It wouldn't surprise me. These guys look like they know something."

They lapsed into silence. Ten minutes went by. Nick went to the window. "Maybe they're trying to reach us and the telephone isn't working."

Marina picked up the room telephone. It was working.

Fifteen minutes passed, during which time they argued about whether they were being secretly observed. It didn't really matter. At the end of a half hour they both realized that, for whatever reason, they had been stood up. No one was coming.

Marina was both relieved and disappointed.

"So what do we do now? Go home?"

Nick's voice mirrored his disappointment. "What else can we do? We have no way to find them. Something must have scared them off. Maybe they picked up on that van of Murdoch's."

Mechanically, they put the chairs back and left the room. They walked back along the long hall and rang for the elevator. They stood hand in hand in the glass cage and let it take them to the lobby.

Suddenly Marina was in tears. She felt as if she had just taken a test and had arrived at the answer after the bell rang.

"They're gone. They called us to meet them and then changed their minds or they knew all along they weren't going to show. And they must have known about Murdoch and Spenser and the others tapping the phone, too. They threw *them* off the trail, too. Now we'll never get them. And we'll never find the peregrines."

Nick gave her hand a warning squeeze. "Shh." He steered her out of the elevator and toward the door. He leaned over and put his arm around her and bent his head toward hers.

"I know. That's what I think, too. But let's not talk about it here. Let's just walk quietly toward the exit, in case they're watching us. We're dealers, remember. It won't do to get emotional."

Out on the steps, Nick and Marina tried unobstrusively to spot the unmarked van. It was nowhere in sight. Nick gave his parking stub to the attendant. It seemed to take forever for him to bring the familiar white Land Rover. And then another eternity passed while he held the door for Marina and then stepped around to the other side of the car to hold it open for Nick. Nick slid in quickly.

"Thank you. This is for you." He held out the tip, his foot already on the accelerator.

"Thank you, sir." But instead of turning away, the attendant leaned in the window. "Certainly is a nice night. Which way you folks heading now?"

Marina could feel Nick's body language. It was saying,

Be careful. He said casually, "Well, we're just heading home. Up to Serenity."

The attendant seemed in no hurry to take his elbows off the windowsill. "You might want to stay off the freeway. Been a bad accident up that way and it's all jammed up. You'd do better on McAlister Road."

Nick shifted gears.

"Is that so? Thanks for the advice. Now, if you'll excuse me . . ." His foot came down on the accelerator and suddenly they were off in a squeal of tires.

Marina looked back at the white-jacketed attendant standing in the middle of the parking lot.

"Hey! You almost bowled that guy over," Marina said.

"Maybe I should have," Nick said. "He was trying to hold us here. And he's probably the guy who tipped them off about the police van, too."

As soon as he said it Marina knew it to be true. But why?

The answer hit them both at the same time, but Marina was the one to say it. "They're leaving the country. Now. Tonight. With the birds. We frightened them off."

"We didn't. It was Murdoch's boys and those Fish and Wildlife cowboys. How could they have been so *dumb*! After we set it up so carefully."

But Marina was not one to waste time on postmortems. "Hey, Nick, pull over for a minute."

Nick obediently pulled off the highway and turned on his flashers.

"Where do you think they've gone?" Marina asked him. "Do you think they're headed for the border?"

Nick sagged; he rested his forehead against the wheel.

"I don't think so," he said. "They wouldn't want to run the risk of a chase. And they know Fish and Wildlife has people who are monitoring and checking borders. I think they'll want to be quick and clean."

"Then let's go, Nick."

"Go where?"

"To the airport!"

CHAPTER

18

ABOUT THE TIME MARINA AND NICK WERE speeding to the airport, a man stood at the glass window of Gate 14 and searched the darkness.

That would be the plane taxiing in. Good. Iberia—yes, that must be it. It would mean a little switching around to go from there to Riyadh, but that was precisely what made this flight desirable.

He glanced up at the sky. No problem with weather. He remembered one flight he had made from Alaska, on the way home with the gyrfalcons. That had been a trip! Ticking off his concerns one by one, he felt in his jacket pocket for the tickets and was comforted by their awkward bulk. One for her, one for him, three for the cargo. Some people might think it foolish to pay for a seat for each of three wooden crates. But he intended to keep the birds with him. He didn't want them banging around in some cargo hold or up in the overhead. Any birds worth that much money deserved to go first class.

Besides, they would need to be fed. Fatima could do it. He hated the nasty, smelly little creatures. He found it demeaning to tend to their needs. But she didn't seem to mind. Perhaps it was because she loved money so much. And these birds were money, as gilt-edged as any bonds. Well, they had certainly worked for it this time.

Those fitted bird boxes that Kallim designed had certainly come in handy. In fact, Kallim had come in handy. Too bad he had gotten hurt in that car crash. He felt he could depend on Kallim not to talk. But anyhow, it didn't matter now. This was his last trip. He and Fatima were getting out.

It is the way of fate, he thought. *If we had not tried to make a final sale, we would have been home by now. The Americans say, Quit while you're ahead.*

That's what I should have done.

Fatima. Where was she? He looked at his watch. She had been in the ladies' room long enough.

As if in answer to his thought, a stout, dark-haired woman in a long skirt and boots sauntered toward him.

She joined him at the window. Behind them, lines formed as people surged through the long corridors from the customs and passport check-in lines.

The Phoenix airport was crowded, as usual. And as usual the roadways that led to it were glutted, even though it was not rush hour. This fact gave Abdul Massuad additional comfort. There was no way that Menaker and the girl would figure out where he was before he left. And even if they did, they couldn't get here in time. Once he was in the air . . . There was the comforting feeling that they had not been followed. Soon they and the falcons would be flying to Malaga and then to Riyadh.

He motioned Fatima toward the seat where the three boxes stood waiting to be carried on to the plane. He looked at his watch again. They should be boarding right now. And then the announcement came.

"All passengers for Iberia flight 509 to Malaga, that plane will be delayed for takeoff at least one hour. We're sorry for any inconvenience. If you leave the boarding area, please check periodically with the overhead schedule printout and listen for further announcements."

Massuad half stood up, then slumped back into the cold molded plastic. It was very important at this time not to react, not to create a scene or in any way draw attention to himself. He and Fatima exchanged a look. Silently he offered her a cigarette, took one himself.

He hadn't anticipated the plane's being delayed. He'd better put a good face on it, for Fatima's sake. She looked distraught.

He spoke to her in Arabic.

"By the time they think to look for us, we'll be gone." But honesty compelled a qualifier.

"Nevertheless, we are now somewhat at risk. Keep your eyes and ears open."

Massuad leaned back and tried to relax.

Perhaps it would all turn out for the best: The boy at the hotel could have been wrong about the unmarked police

146

van. Maybe Menaker would have been a supplier as well as a buyer. It would have been good to have an additional contact before he left. He could have sold the name in Riyadh, even without the birds.

Quit while you're ahead. We'll see.

Nick and Marina raced toward the airport.

"If it hadn't been for that parking attendant, I would never have thought they were trying to hold us there. They must have paid him off to watch for us."

"I'm still not sure. And when we get there, how are we going to know where to start to look? There are international flights leaving every night and we don't know where they're headed."

"We'll check 'em out one by one. All we can do is try."

Marina shook her head.

"It's too big a job. We need help. There's a phone booth. Pull over for a minute and let me call Murdoch and tell him what we're doing."

"Where in blazes are they, anyway? Some backup."

Nick brought the car to a screeching stop.

"They're probably wondering where we are."

"Make it snappy."

Marina jumped out of the car and ran to the booth.

She opened her handbag.

Oh, no. No quarters. Wouldn't you know.

She ran back and got a coin from Nick.

She dialed the number. "We're sorry, the number you have dialed is out of service at this time."

It couldn't be. It was the number they had given her—

147

the number in the van. She must have dialed it wrong. This is like one of those frustration nightmares. She tried again, with Nick waving frantically at her.

Ah! Now it was ringing.

"Yes?" It was Murdoch's voice.

"Hello. Mr. Murdoch? This is Marina Cassidy."

Breathlessly, she laid out the situation for Murdoch. Meanwhile, Nick was fulminating. Finally he got out of the car and came over toward the booth. His face looked gray and drawn and she noticed that he was favoring his bad leg more than usual.

She hung up, after getting Murdoch's assurance that they would meet them at the airport.

"That was too much time," said Nick sharply.

"Okay, okay. What's wrong with your foot?"

"I think I did something to it pressing on the accelerator. I'm in pain."

"I'll drive." Marina slipped into the driver's seat before Nick could protest.

She started the motor.

"I didn't know you had a license."

"I don't. Learner's permit. It will have to do."

Nick nodded.

"I'll shift," he said. "Go!"

Ten minutes later they were at the airport. Marina drove the car into the first parking lot she could find and she raced ahead of Nick up the escalator and followed the signs to the international flights. But—abruptly—she realized how hopeless it was. They had no way to proceed beyond the barriers. No passports. Nothing.

148

Nick caught up with her. He looked around and immediately sized up the situation.

He groaned. "All the times I've traveled, and I forgot about this. The police will be able to get in. But we'll have to wait."

It was the most excruciating agony to be there and be so impotent.

"We can at least check out the flights," Nick said. "Come on." They raced over to the computer monitor.

It was the ultimate frustration to read about the flight to Tel Aviv that was still listed but had left ten minutes ago.

"There are two flights that haven't gone out. One is a flight to Amsterdam that leaves in about thirty minutes. The other is a flight to Spain that's being delayed. They could be on either one. But my hunch is they left on the Israeli flight."

"We'll never know."

"We might," said a voice.

Murdoch had come up behind them quietly.

"After you called, we did our homework. Thanks to the computer age, we were able to check all the passenger lists. A few sound promising, notably one Abdul Massuad, who is traveling with a female companion and has bought three extra seats for his luggage! The plane was being held but is now ready for takeoff. However, they are holding the boarding for us. Let's go."

The tall slim man wearing the expensive suit did not fit Marina's mental image of an international bird thief. First of all, he was outrageously handsome. And his indignation at being searched seemed genuine. His female companion, too, didn't fit Marina's idea of a criminal. *That idea of the criminal type*, Marina thought somewhat later, *is a notion I must revise.*

Because Abdul Massuad and Fatima Dhibal, handsome and polite as they seemed, *were* the international falcon smugglers. If there was any doubt about it, the three young peregrine falcons with false bands on their legs in custom-built crates confirmed it.

And one of the birds was pure white.

CHAPTER

19

"I CAN'T BELIEVE IT," ISABEL SAID.

Marina and Nick were sitting in the Cassidy kitchen eating Isabel's enchiladas and filling her in on what had happened.

"What can't you believe?"

Isabel poured herself a cup of coffee and sat down. "Start at the beginning once again. You are throwing everything at me too fast."

Nick broke in eagerly.

"What's hard to believe is that we caught the smugglers and we saved the peregrines."

Marina's laugh bubbled.

"Truth is, *Mamacita*, if I'd written that story I would never have given it such a pat ending. It's almost too good to be true to have it wrap up so neatly."

Isabel regarded the young people serenely.

"By neatly you mean that you have also caught Jimmy Toddy's murderer. *Verdad?*"

Nick and Marina looked up, surprised that Isabel had put it in the form of a question.

Nick said, "Well, yeah. Sure. I mean they had the birds. They had to have done it."

"Aren't they still investigating?"

"Well, yes, but that's only a formality."

And Marina said, "Come on, Ma, don't start that again."

Isabel looked into her coffee cup. "Don't let us jump to confusions," she said.

Marina and Nick hooted. "Conclusions, Ma."

"Confusions is what I meant," Isabel said firmly.

"Well, anyway," she said, getting up. "The main thing is you two are safe. I was very worried. Now. How about finishing that last enchilada, *muchachos?*"

The sorting-out process took awhile. There were meetings with lawyers and sworn statements taken and postmortems about evidence and sequence of events.

But when it was all over, the plot that Marina had thought was so neat still had a large hole. There was not a shred of evidence linking either Abdul Massuad or Fatima Dhibal to the murder of Jimmy Toddy.

In fact, both of them had airtight alibis. They also had good connections. Their embassy immediately began negotiations designed to keep them out of United States courts. Because the case threatened to become an international incident, it was quietly disposed of. Within a few weeks the two falcon smugglers were on their way to Riyadh. This time they went nonstop.

Marina and Nick were bitterly disappointed.

"They're getting away with murder," was Marina's personal verdict.

Nick used it as an example of the unfairness of the whole United States justice system.

Isabel kept her own counsel.

When everything had been taken care of, Sam Spenser and the Fish and Wildlife investigators pulled out of Serenity, leaving Murdoch and the police, Cheryl, Nick, Marina, and Isabel with the central question: Who had murdered Jimmy Toddy?

As they went over and over the evidence, certain facts stood out. Massuad and his companion were near the top of the smuggling ring. But there were still many others, as yet unidentified, who were dealing illegally in rare birds. In fact, the birds in Massuad's possession had been bought from someone who had put leg bands on them so that it would appear that they had been bred in captivity. All of this argued for the fact that that same person could have taken the peregrines from the nest and killed Toddy. But how?

These loose ends dangled maddeningly for Marina. She chewed over the puzzle endlessly. She was driving Isabel "loco."

Several days later Murdoch called them all together at Cheryl's. He went over the details once again.

"You mean there's nothing that links Massuad to the nest on Montenegro?"

"That's right. Neither my staff nor any of the Fish and Wildlife investigators have turned up a shred of evidence on the murder or on whom Massuad got those birds from. There appears to be no connection between Massuad and company and whoever killed Jimmy Toddy. And it was greed that drove Massuad to contact Nick, not any special connection with the platinum peregrine and its offspring."

"I wouldn't be surprised if old Sam had a hand in this," Nick said.

Cheryl snapped at him.

"What is that supposed to mean? I can vouch for Sam. He and I go back a long way."

"I'll bet."

Cheryl shot Nick a look that told him he was off base.

"Sam is kind of rough cut, but he's a good guy, basically. Got into trouble, made a few mistakes. Like some other people I know."

Nick dropped the subject of Sam Spenser temporarily. But Marina knew he had planted an idea in Murdoch's head—an idea she was sure would be thoroughly checked out, even though the portly policeman was announcing that the case was about to be closed.

"You mean, you're going to give up on Jimmy Toddy's murder?"

"That's about it," Murdoch admitted. "I can't put anything together."

Neither can I, Marina admitted. It was like writing the plot for a story, and not being able to quite work out the ending.

The difference was that in a story you could change the

facts. In real life you were stuck with them.

Once again, she went over in her mind what they knew. There had been a murder. *Fact.* The birds were sold. *Another fact.* Start with what you know, à la Arnheim. And then—use it as a springboard. Depart. Take off.

Suddenly, she had it.

"Hey! Maybe we should separate them."

"Separate whom?"

"The two facts. I mean, maybe they're not connected in the way we've been thinking they are. Maybe Jimmy Toddy wasn't killed by a bird smuggler. Maybe he was murdered by someone else, for a totally different reason."

Murdoch stopped sighing.

"That's a possibility," he agreed. "Something personal, like jealousy over a woman. Or—even more likely—a problem between a Native American who's sworn to protect the environment and some tribal custom that goes against it. And if we're saying that the birds weren't involved in the murder, then it opens up a whole new line of thinking."

"Like what?" Nick wasn't buying this new angle so fast.

"Like the fact that Massuad claims his contact got the peregrines as *eggs* and hatched them. If he's not lying, that would mean that the eggs were taken *before* Jimmy Toddy knew they were there and staked out the mountain."

One thing Marina knew: She had to get back up that mountain. She itched to see the peregrine pair once again and to try to find out what had happened to that last eyass. And maybe there was a clue to the murder somewhere on that precipice.

She told Nick what she was planning.

"Let me know when you want to go, and I'll drive you out there."

But Marina said, "Nick, do you mind? I'd like to go alone."

"I do mind. I want to come. What's the matter, are you afraid I'll slow you down?"

Marina was horrified that he should think that. She had forgotten about his foot. She put her face in his shoulder and said in a muffled voice, "That's not it. I just want to go and make my peace with the place. I haven't been there since—since it all happened. I need to get it straight in my mind. For the story."

Nick put his arms around her.

"For the story? You still trying to tie up all the loose ends for a story for old Arnheim?"

"Well, sort of. Maybe more for myself than for him. Leaving it hanging bugs me. At least if I go back maybe I'll think of a way to end it. It seems so unsatisfactory this way."

"I don't think you should go," Nick said.

"You can't tell me what to do, Nick."

"Yeah. I know. But Isabel can. I'm gonna tell," he said, forcing a grin.

"No, you're not. You'll be quiet and wait for me at the house. I'll go early and be home by noon."

Nick knew when he was beaten.

The next morning Marina was up before dawn. She dressed, ate an orange, filled a canteen with water, and set out for the beacon of Montenegro. Her senses seemed sharpened by the morning air. The desert had never seemed more alive. There were the familiar Harris hawks. There went a lone coyote, loping down the arroyo, spooking a great horned owl out of a cottonwood tree. She felt like shouting for joy. Everything was the same, or even more beautiful than she remembered it. She realized that she had been afraid that the experience—Jimmy Toddy's murder and the smuggling of the birds—would have put a curse on the place, and that at the base of Montenegro there would be some reminder, like a mark of Cain. But there was nothing. The mountain was as it had always been.

Marina looked up toward the summit. She knew she needed to go up once more. This time she was prepared. She had on studded boots and heavy gloves.

She started up, clambering toward the narrow observation point. And finally she was there once again, staring through the crack of gray rock where the story had begun.

There was the remnant of nest. A few fluffy bird feathers that still clung to the sticks and some dried dribble of whiting marked the place where the birds had used the shelf for a landing platform . . . nothing more.

She swept the area with her glasses, looking for a sign of falcons in the sky or perched on a distant ledge. The mountain was deserted.

And then she saw the shape of a peregrine, swooping down from a great height, diving toward a clump of brush. She watched as it brought down the quail with one powerful rap of its feet and then pulled it into the tall grass to eat.

It was an immature peregrine. She could tell by its size, by its choice of prey, and by its speckled breast. But in the rest of it, the bird had taken after its mother. The last of the four was pure platinum!

Satisfied that she had seen what she had come to see, Marina made the final trip down Montenegro, thinking about the bird.

What a beauty! It'll be on its first passage flight south soon. Probably wind up in Argentina.

Hey. Pact, she told herself. *Let's not tell anyone about this one, okay? No one but Nick, that is, and Isabel.*

She grinned to herself, the falcon a warm force around her, mantling her secret.

Full of the beauty of the peregrine, Marina strolled toward home. It was full morning now, and hot as usual. Drowsily, she reviewed the events of the past weeks.

Sometimes I feel guilty—I wanted so much to have some-thing happen *in Serenity. But I didn't wish for someone to get killed. It's like the fairy tale about the three wishes. There's always a flaw in the bargain; if you get one thing you wish for, you get something else along with it.*

She imagined Nick arguing with her.

You didn't make that death happen, Marina.

About one hundred and fifty feet from the base of Mon-tenegro, Marina detoured toward a clump of small acacia trees. She was following her long-established ritual— checking out the pack rat. She had watched the pack rat's midden, or nest, grow over a period of a year, but had never seen the creature itself. Still, she knew it was around somewhere, collecting the assortment of shiny objects for which it had a penchant. Each time Marina looked at the mound there was something new there—a wad of aluminum foil left by a careless picnicker, a bottle top, a piece of shiny glass. *What a junk heap!* she thought. She wondered where Señor Pack Rat kept himself. Was there an entrance down there? As Marina bent down to give the midden a closer inspection, a particularly bright glint caught her eye. Reluctant to put her bare hand into the pile, she drew on her gloves again and dislodged the sticks that partly covered the object.

The sticks fell away. Now Marina could see that it was a metal army dog tag.

Unmindful now of danger, Marina reached down swiftly and pulled it out.

The name on the tag was clear.

Leroy Bob Parvin. And there was a serial number.

Marina cupped the sun-warmed medallion in her hand and stood quietly in the white hot light of the desert. Of all the things she had thought might happen on this trip, this was the event she could least have predicted. And somehow she had a gut feeling that the tag she had found was connected with the events that had occurred around Montenegro. Whoever owned this tag was either connected with the birds or—with Jimmy Toddy.

With a sudden jolt of fear, she looked up, half expecting Leroy Bob Parvin to be standing at her elbow. But she was alone.

Resisting the impulse to run, Marina began the walk home.

For the last half mile, she could see Nick in the distance, waiting for her at the edge of the desert, hands on hips.

She waved to him. She clasped her hands above her head in a gesture of victory. The last few hundred yards she ran, and it seemed like a mile.

She showed her treasure to Nick and Isabel. Murdoch was called.

"It may not mean anything," he said. But the tone of his voice said it could mean something, and he didn't sigh. The computers went to work on the life history and whereabouts of one Leroy Bob Parvin.

The computers were quick and efficient.

Murdoch reported.

"He's a white male, age forty-two. Been a drifter, served time for robbery and assault. And get this, boys and girls"—Murdoch's murmurous voice rose—"he was picked up once on suspicion of cactus rustling but there was not enough evidence to convict."

Murdoch took a sip of Isabel's fine *cafe con leche*. He bit thoughtfully into a cruller.

"This puts a whole different light on things," he said. "Suppose for the sake of argument . . ."

Marina jumped in.

"Jimmy Toddy is watching for bird smugglers, and he sees some cactus rustlers instead. He comes down from his hiding place. . . ."

Nick picked up the narrative.

"He's not armed, but he tries to arrest the rustlers. They overpower him, but he puts up a real fight. During that time this guy Parvin drops his dog tags. Someone

160

whacks Jimmy on the head. He's not dead, just unconscious. They realize what they've done. They panic. They
take his shirt, hat, and canteen to make sure the desert
will do him in. They leave him for dead, cover their tracks,
and hightail it out of there."

Now it was Isabel's turn.

"One morning the pack rat is looking for some new fur-
nishing for his house. He finds one of the shiny tags and
carries it back from the base of Montenegro to his midden."

"It's a plausible plot."

Murdoch pushed his chair away from the table and stood
up.

"And now, boys and girls, we have to find him."

It took four weeks to locate Leroy Bob Parvin. But it
took only four hours to extract a confession from him. He
had killed Jimmy Toddy, and it had happened pretty much
the way they had imagined.

Nick and Marina were sitting in the Land Rover, watching the sun go down, and rehashing their favorite subject—
the sting and its aftermath.

"Did you ever think when we met in Arnheim's class
that it would turn out like this?"

"Not really. I certainly didn't think you were the kind of
girl who went out looking for trouble!"

"Not trouble. Experience."

Marina shivered. "You know, that first day I went up the
mountain Isabel gave me a really hard time about being
out here alone. One of the things she mentioned was plant
rustlers."

"See. You should always listen to your mother."

"Yeah. Well, one thing I've learned from this, anyway."

"What's that? Or do you want to save it for one of your stories?"

"No, I can tell you. It goes like this. Will and I shared the bird-watching thing. I guess I unconsciously wanted to keep it going. But—the thing is—there's more to life than just observing. You can't want things to happen just so you can observe them. You have to somehow bring something of yourself to it. I think that's what Isabel was trying to tell me when she said I should put myself *in the way* of experience. I think she meant—keep your eyes open and be a part of it, too. Then, if you want to write about it, you'll have something. And I do. I want to be a writer. I know that now."

"Get a load of that sunset." Nick seemed to be changing the subject. They watched the spectacular reds and oranges turn pink and purple.

He finally said, "It's a powerful lesson, to be involved with something and then realize that other things are more important. I think I learned that, too. That's why I—I think I'll hack Roxanne back to the wild, if I can. I'd rather think of her roaming free, hunting on her own. Flying falcons suddenly isn't that important to me. Especially since my girl doesn't like it."

The sun had set. Nick reached over and took Marina's hand.

"I saw you the first day you came to class. One look and I had memorized you, as if you were a new bird I'd never seen before . . . the way your hair rippled down your back and those dopey sandals you wore that kept making that

162

clopping sound whenever you moved your feet. Sitting in front of you I could smell that perfume or whatever it is you wear. I used to try to lean back a little so I could catch it. Did you notice?"

"No."

His voice was low.

"I thought you were the most attractive girl I had ever seen. But I figured there must be a big long line, and I'd have to start all the way at the end of it, so . . ."

Marina felt a surge of energy.

"That's just like you, Nick Menaker! Always want to be first or you won't play. Little did you know that there was no one else on the line, so you were guaranteed first place."

"Hey, lady, you telling me I'm winning the sweepstakes because there are no other horses running?"

"That's about it," she said, suddenly confident.

Nick took her in his arms and held her for a long time, while he murmured against her hair, "I don't want to win you or tame you or anything like that. I don't even care if you don't like my Harley."

He kissed her until she was breathless.

After a while, Marina said, "I guess I'd better be getting home. Isabel will be worried."

"Nah, she won't," he said, grinning. "I already told her we might be late."

BARBARA BRENNER and her husband, wildlife artist Fred Brenner, have been to the Southwest and Mexico many times, exploring the terrain and studying the wildlife, especially the birds.

The author's deep interest in the relationships between people and animals in today's world is seen in such outstanding books as *A Killing Season* and *The Gorilla Signs Love*. She has also written *On The Frontier with Mr. Audubon*, chosen by *School Library Journal* as one of the "Best of the Best Books."

For many years, Barbara Brenner has been encouraging young people to write, through workshops she has given for students in elementary, high school, and college classes.

The Brenners live in Lords Valley, Pennsylvania.